Subtle DECEIT

Peace & Blessings

Alma

ALMA L. DAVEY

Wasteland Press
www.wastelandpress.net
Shelbyville, KY USA

Subtle Deceit
by Alma L. Davey

Copyright © 2015 Alma L. Davey
ALL RIGHTS RESERVED

First Printing – August 2015
ISBN: 978-1-68111-050-9
Cover design by: Sandra Ballenger, Graphic Designer
www.sandraballenger.com

Scripture quotations marked KJV are from *The Holy Bible, King James Version*. Copyright © 1994 by The Zondervan Corporation, all rights reserved.

This book is strictly a fictional writing. The characters, places, names and incidents are taken from the author's imagination and any resemblance to real people, places or situations are purely coincidental and unintentional. Any mention of products or businesses is not for advertisement or promotional purposes, but to enhance the particular passage of the writing.

NO PART OF THIS BOOK MAY BE REPRODUCED IN ANY FORM, BY PHOTOCOPYING OR BY ANY ELECTRONIC OR MECHANICAL MEANS, INCLUDING INFORMATION STORAGE OR RETRIEVAL SYSTEMS, WITHOUT PERMISSION IN WRITING FROM THE COPYRIGHT OWNER/AUTHOR

Printed in the U.S.A.

0   1   2   3   4   5   6   7

ACKNOWEDGEMENTS

All of the glory belongs to God for the writing of this book. I thank Him for the mandate He placed on me to pen this book and for the guidance of the Holy Spirit. I thank God for all of the people that He directed into my life to help, encourage and love me through the years that it took me to complete this writing, which was written at a very difficult time in my life.

Thanks to Patricia Haley, best-selling author, friend and encourager for believing in me and imparting her wisdom, knowledge and compassion throughout this writing journey.

Thanks to my dear granddaughters Alyse and Adriana. Alyse frequently reminded me that I was behind schedule and Adriana read portions of the unfinished work to give me her opinion and thoughts.

Thanks to Jennifer Gooch, Reverend Joyce B. Calvin, and Terri Irumondomon who saw my gift to write long before I received it. Thank you for helping me to discover my gift, encouraging me and insisting that I use this God given gift.

To all who sowed generously your love, prayers, time and resources so that I could complete this book: Lou B. Colbert (sister and #1 cheerleader), Raphel and Martha Watson (niece and husband), Lillie Banks (niece), Gloria Harris, DeLisa Scott, Sobrina Hampton, Sherrill Escartin, Michael Mayo, Pamela Little, Rochelle Cowley, Susie Sanders, Antionette Bryant, Mary McCain, and Rodney and Debra Brown.

I'm so grateful to Jennifer Gooch and Alphonso Butler III for using their fashion knowledge to assist me in dressing my characters and giving me interior design tips for several of the rooms in the story.

Because of all of you, this book has become a reality and I pray it will be a blessing to all who reads it.

Trust in the Lord with all thine heart; and lean not to thine own understanding. In all thy ways acknowledge him, and he shall direct thy paths.
(Proverbs 3:5-6)

CHAPTER ONE

Candace extended her hand inviting Jessica to follow her down the aisle to be seated in the church sanctuary. The thought of turning around and exiting the church crossed her mind as Candace gestured for her to be seated and handed her a program.

I saved this seat just for you," Candace said.

Jessica took a deep breath and let out a long sigh as she sat down, wishing the sick feeling in her stomach would go away. She hoped her attire met with the church folk's approval. Draped on her forearm was the jacket to her perfect size ten baby blue dress that hugged her hips and belled out as it got to the hemline and ended midway her knee, exposing her long shapely legs. The cushioned bench was a welcome change to the wooden benches she remembered as a young girl. The choir began to sing and the congregation stood to join them. "Oh give thanks unto the Lord," sang the man next to Jessica, loud and off key.

Church—Is this a good place for me to change my life? I don't know where to begin. God doesn't know me and I certainly don't know him. I don't belong here among these good spiritual people. God is probably thinking that I have a lot of nerve coming to his house. I shouldn't have let Candace talk me into coming. There is no hope for me here.

"Excuse me," a man said, as he shuffled down the row. Jessica turned her body to the side to let him pass. The scent of his cologne reminded her of the man she was struggling to forget.

"Welcome to Mercy Seat, Jesus loves you," he said to Jessica.

The entire congregation was repeating the welcome to each other. She was able to get a better look at Mr. Smelling Good when they took up the offering. He was very good looking; about her age, early forties, approximately five feet, eleven inches tall and one hundred eighty-five pounds. He had a well-groomed fade haircut and mustache. There was no wedding band on his hand. So far Jessica liked what she saw. She didn't really approve of men wearing earrings, but the small diamond in his ear looked good on him.

"Please open your Bible to the book of John, chapter 3, verse 16," the preacher said.

Jessica fumbled through the pages of the Bible she borrowed from Candace. Everyone stood and read aloud. *For God so loved the world that he gave his only begotten son, that whosoever believeth in him, shall not perish, but have everlasting life.*

"Please be seated. My topic for today is *God's Unconditional Love for Us*. He loves each of you regardless of who you are. He doesn't like some of the things we do because they don't agree with his word, yet he still loves us; so much that he came to earth in the form of a man and gave himself as a sacrificial offering on the cross for our sins. Would any of you give your child's life for someone else, especially when you know things about them that are not good?"

He paused to scan the sanctuary to see the reaction of the congregation before he continued. "That is unconditional love."

Shouts of amen and hallelujahs rang out. The lady sitting next to Jessica elbowed a man who had his eyes closed and his head was bobbing up and down as he tried to keep from falling off the bench. Jessica checked her watch, crossed her legs and folded her arms.

This sermon couldn't be for me. Why would God love me or sacrifice his son for me with all of the things that I've done? What does God want from me? I'm not sure what I want from him, but if he is who people say he is, perhaps there is hope for me.

The church service was over and Jessica exited to meet Candace in the parking lot. Candace appeared looking a few inches taller than she had during church service. She had replaced her navy blue wedge loafers that she wore with her usher uniform with three inch heels.

"I'm hungry, let's go eat," Candace said. "How did you enjoy the church service? Reverend Anderson preached a great message and the choir really sang today. Don't you agree?"

Jessica couldn't answer one question before she asked the other.

"Let's head over to Mandy's. They have the best fried chicken in town you know."

Jessica loved Candace, but there were times when she got on her nerves with her fast talking and controlling attitude.

"I enjoyed the service," Jessica replied, with one hand on her hip mimicking Candace. "The preacher was good and I really enjoyed the choir."

Candace walked toward her car ignoring Jessica's obvious irritation with her. I'm so hungry I could eat a horse or at least a few chickens."

"Looks like you already have my afternoon planned for me, so let's go eat," Jessica said. She knew it was useless to try to have a conversation with Candace while her mind was on food.

"Good afternoon ladies. How are you today?"

Jessica looked up from her menu at the tall dark skinned man with close cut greying hair and beard in his middle to late fifties. She always liked to look into the eyes of a man to see what he really looked like, but he was wearing Carrera Aviator glasses, making it impossible to see his eyes. He wore a black Burberry suit with a white shirt, a Burberry tie and pocket square and Gucci loafers. She knew a well-dressed man when she saw one. Keith taught her a lot about the popular fashion designs for men and women. He made sure she wore the best when she was with him and he always looked great. She was truly going to miss being able to shop at the best places now that they were no longer a couple. Designer clothes were not affordable on her salary.

Her attention was drawn back to the stranger standing before her as his thick lips parted in a captivating smile revealing a nice set if pearly whites.

"Hail, hail the King has arrived," Candace said sarcastically.

"Sister Candace, it's good to see you. I see you are evangelizing. Who is your pretty friend?"

"I'm Jessica Jones," she said, reaching out to shake his hand.

He extended his hand to meet hers revealing his manicured nails and a diamond pinky ring. The time on his wrist was noticeably displayed by his two-toned diamond bezel Movado watch.

"It's a pleasure to meet you Jessica. I'm King Jordan. I saw you in church today and I hope you will visit us again and get involved. We need good teachers and I believe that you would make a good one."

The last person Candace wanted to entertain was King and she certainly didn't want him zooming in on Jessica. What she knew of him was not good and she knew this was not someone that Jessica should get involved with.

"Okay King," Candace interrupted, "you've met her, now we'd like to enjoy our meal without the presence of the quack prophet."

"Candace, it's always a pleasure. Pretty lady, we will meet again."

"I'm sure we will Mr. King, Jessica said as he walked away. She felt bad that Candace had spoken to him so harshly. He was very polite and she didn't want him to think she agreed with Candace's rudeness. A frown covered Candace's face.

"Mr. King! Puh-leese! King is his name, but a king he is not. I suggest you stay as far away from him as possible."

"Why? He seems like a nice person, very pleasant and not bad looking," Jessica said, turning to look in the direction he was walking. He was still close enough to hear Candace who was still speaking in her usual loud voice.

"He's always getting into everybody's business; you know, a nosy body," Candace continued. "Nobody knows much about him, but he seems to know a lot about everybody else. I just avoid him like a badly dressed man trying to come on to me and I suggest you do the same."

"I don't understand. What kind of things does he know about people? What does he know about you for instance?"

"Jessica, I really don't want to talk about King Jordan. He's just bad news. Some people say that he has a gift that allows him to tell you things about your life. I say he's gifted at getting into other folks business. Just be careful; I can tell by the gleam in his eyes that you are surely on his hit list."

"Candace, he had on dark glasses, so how could you possibly see a gleam in his eyes?"

"Oh, you know what I mean. For someone who has been out in the world all of your life, how could you miss it? Honey I can see right through men like him. Trust me, his eyes were gleaming and the wheels of his mind were turning like the propellers on a jet airplane." Candace's voice escalated and people began to stare at them.

Jessica was surprised at Candace's tone of voice. "Wow, he must have really found your goat and untied it. You seem almost angry with him. Come on girl, now you have me curious. What did he say to get you so angry? Did you have a fling with the King? "Jessica said laughing, something she hadn't done in the last few months. "How come you never told me about him? Come on Candace, tell me about King." Jessica looked at Candace with a smirk on her face.

"I told you, I don't want to discuss King. He's nobody, just a trouble maker." Candace placed her elbow on the table and put her hand under her chin. "You see, he's already got us going at each other for no reason. Just drop it Jessica."

Jessica had almost forgotten about her problem while she was trying to have some innocent fun with Candace, but the fun was over. She could see that Candace was serious and continuing to probe her about King was not a good idea.

The waitress came to take their orders and Candace breathed a sigh of relief.

CHAPTER TWO

Jessica parked her car and walked towards her condo. She could feel the multi-colored leaves crunching under her feet. The children playing ball, the birds chirping and the beautiful sunset made it almost a perfect fall day.

She hadn't been to church for over twenty years, and her visit to Mercy Seat turned out better than she anticipated. The people made her feel welcome, but she felt so unworthy to sit in God's house. She wondered if they could see beyond her smile into her hurt and anger. She wasn't sure if she would be going back again. Stopping to eat with Candace was almost a good idea, until the episode with King. Candace and God were the only two people who knew about her recent problem and neither of them had helped her feel better about it today.

She entered her apartment and sat in the big chair by the window watching the children still trying to capture a few more minutes of playtime. The past four months had been hell, or what she imagined hell to be like. She had been hurt by the last person she expected. It was hard not to think about Keith. Before she met him, her life had been filled with one relationship after another and some were only one night stands that she didn't always recall their names. Meeting Keith was like breathing a breath of fresh air.

They met at The Spider Web, a popular night club that she occasionally went to for a night of fun. It was a Halloween costume party and Jessica was dressed as Little Red Riding Hood. Keith was in town on business and was invited by a client. His work as a self-employed corporate attorney brought him to Chicago often. Jessica was not at all disappointed that he was not wearing a costume, because he looked great as himself. They were instantly attracted to each other. When they started dating, he made special trips to Chicago just to see Jessica. Unlike his predecessors, he actually took her out on dates to dinner, movies and parties. He was smart, good looking, hard-working, and treated her like a queen; lavishing her with expensive gifts. They had begun to talk about marriage, so she thought she had finally met the man that would take her away from the never ending cycle of looking for Mr. Right.

She often traveled with him to various cities. When they went to Detroit where he lived, they always stayed in a hotel because he said he wanted uninterrupted time with her. He told her that he lived with his invalid mother who had a live in nurse and housekeeper, but she had met his two brothers and a few other relatives at a barbeque at his brother's home. They always communicated by cell phone and she could always reach him.

She was preparing for bed one night after her usual one hour phone chat with him, when the phone rang. The caller ID showed Keith's name, but it was not his cell number. On the other end was a woman's voice that told her she was Keith's wife of eight years. They lived in a suburb of Detroit with their two children; six and two years old. She had known about Jessica for almost a year and Keith had promised that he would dissolve the relationship three months ago. When she saw from his cell phone bill that he was still talking to Jessica every day, she knew he had not kept his word. Jessica was surprised at the calmness in her voice as she told her that this was not the first or second time that she had made a call like this. The last thing she said before hanging up was, "I forgive you." Jessica knew she had to end her relationship with Keith, but it was easier said than done. She just wanted to kill him and then maybe the pain, hurt and anger would go away. Not even Oxycodone could help ease the pain she was feeling. Her heart felt as if it was broken into pieces.

The phone rang and Jessica, awakening to a dark room, reached over to turn on the lamp. It was around three o'clock in the afternoon when she arrived home and now the clock said six. She checked the caller ID before answering. This was a time that she hoped the caller ID could be wrong. She hesitated, then slowly picked up the phone and placed it to her ear without speaking.

"Jessica, please talk to me," the voice on the other end said. "I love you. We can work this out. Renee has agreed to give me a divorce and we can get married just as we planned. Please say something."

Jessica took a deep breath and screamed into the phone. "Lies, lies and more lies. I don't think I can ever trust you or any other man again."

"But Jessica—"

"Keith, I believed you really loved me. You lied to me. You have a wife and children. She said you've had other affairs."

"Jessica, I do love you," he interrupted.

"This can't continue. You flew back and forth from Detroit for two years; deceiving me the entire time." She disconnected the call and threw the phone across the room. "No more phone calls from Mr. Keith Blake," she screamed as the tears ran down her face.

Hanging up the phone didn't make her stop thinking about him. No matter what she did, he was still on her mind and in her heart. Even the picture on the night stand was there to remind her of him. He had the smoothest skin she had ever seen on a man. His mustache and hair were cut to perfection, always looking as if he just stepped from the barber's chair. That baby blue T-shirt he wore really accentuated his six feet muscular body. His long bowed legs gave a new meaning to a pair of jeans. She threw the eight by ten inch picture to the floor and stomped it with her foot. "You're not wonderful, you're awful. You're a liar and I hate you." She threw herself across the bed sobbing until she fell asleep.

CHAPTER THREE

Candace reached over to hit the snooze alarm for the third time. Monday morning was her favorite time to take off or go in late, but she had run out of believable excuses. She held on to the pillow as if it would save her from the path she needed to take to get from the bed to the hospital where she worked as a lab technician. The voice on the radio rang out with an old song that Candace used to love entitled *Master Can You Use Me*. This morning she wasn't feeling like God wanted to use her for anything. She felt convicted about her night out. It would definitely be the last date with William.

She met him while waiting to get her car washed and after several phone conversations decided to go to dinner with him. It didn't take long to realize that the six feet three, two hundred seventy-five pound car salesman was full of himself and the amount of food he consumed made it clear why he was a man of sizable stature. The number of drinks he had during dinner certainly didn't bring out the best in him and it became clear to Candace that he was not the kind of man she wanted in her life. He constantly stared at her like a hungry lion ready to pounce on its prey.

"I already know what I want for dessert," he said during dinner, looking her up and down.

She recognized that look in his eyes that she had seen so many times before from men who felt buying you dinner meant going to bed with them was part of the menu. Candace had no intentions of spending another minute with him, especially since he was being very clear about his intentions. She excused herself to go to the ladies room, but exited the restaurant without saying goodbye. She wished she had stayed home and read a good book.

She recalled her mother's wisdom about men. "Choosing a man on looks alone is never good honey," her mother always said. She may have been right, but the choices she had to choose from weren't good. She made the decision to live by God's Word and this meant living a life of celibacy and trusting God to bring the right man into her life. As the years rolled by, she watched other ladies in her age category get married and have children, but she also saw the selection of good, eligible Christian men grow smaller. The competition was overwhelming and God just seemed to have forgotten about her.

Her occasional night out on the town was something that she hadn't shared with Jessica. She also hadn't told Jessica about Albert from Mercy Seat. Many times it crossed her mind to accompany Jessica to night clubs and parties, but the conviction she felt always kept her from following through. She and Jessica had been friends since high school, but she was the one who had been consistent about attending church. Jessica always called her Holy Mama when they were younger. Once she almost envied Jessica because she seemed to be having so much fun, but that changed when she concluded that Jessica had never had a real relationship as long as she had known her. Her relationship with Keith had been the only one that had lasted longer than six months. Now that she had convinced Jessica to come to church, she didn't want to let her know that she had stopped trusting God and sought companionship on her own with Albert, William and others.

She sat up on the side of the bed, holding her head with both hands.

A hot shower and prayer should revive me, she thought, *but God probably has the heavenly phone off the hook so I can't get through.*

She headed for the shower. One look in the mirror at her red eyes with the bags under them told her that she was also in need of a makeover before she faced the world.

CHAPTER FOUR

Candace tried to sneak past her supervisor in route to her work station. She hoped she was out or busy and wouldn't notice her coming in; but just when she thought she had safely passed her office, she called out to her.

"Miss Brown, please see me in my office."

She was only five minutes late, but tardiness was a major issue with Callie. Candace's personnel file was full of write-ups for tardiness. "Good morning Callie," Candace said cheerfully.

"Miss Brown you will be docked for one half hour today. Please be on time tomorrow. I don't like having my schedule disrupted to fill in for you. The patients that come here to Henry North Hospital expect timely service and so do I."

"Yes, of course I will be on time tomorrow," Candace said, trying to sound as reassuring as possible.

"And every day henceforth, if you want to remain employed here," Callie said, looking at Candace over the top of her eyeglasses. Callie wasn't very sympathetic to anyone about being late for work unless you could prove you were near death.

"Absolutely no more tardiness," Candace said.

She knew that if she said much more she would be hitting the pavement looking for a new job. Silence was her best defense.

"Please report to your station immediately Miss Brown."

Candace's great skills as a lab technician had not gone unnoticed. She had been promoted six months ago to assistant supervisor in the lab. This was a big responsibility and she needed to set a better example. Whenever they had a patient that required an expert to draw blood, they called Candace. She knew this was the main reason that Callie hadn't fired her.

When she arrived at the lab, Christine, one of the lab technicians, already had two patients waiting for her.

"Good morning everyone," Candace said to the three people working under her supervision. "Is everything going okay this morning?" Two of them acknowledged that everything was fine.

"Candace, Mr. Hawkins and Miss Albertson are waiting to get their blood drawn. They won't let anyone else do it but you," Christine said.

Candace knew that Christine could be a great technician if she wasn't so afraid and would stop letting the patients intimidate her. She decided today she would assign one of the patients to Christine and stay with her while she drew the blood. "Christine, get your tray and have Mr. Hawkins sit at your station. I'll come over and assist you. We have to be able to service our patients regardless of who is here."

"But, he said," Christine tried to explain to Candace who interrupted her.

"I'll take care of Mr. Hawkins, you just follow my instructions and toughen up and stop being so afraid. You can do this. Now get your tray." Candace was stern with Christine because being sympathetic with her was not helping her become confident in her ability to do her best. She also knew that Mr. Hawkins always asked for her so he could flirt and at the age of seventy-two, close to two hundred pounds and in a wheelchair, along with all of the medical issues he had, flirting was his way of entertaining himself. He was a dirty old man, but today Candace was determined that he would get his blood drawn by Christine.

"Good morning Mr. Hawkins. How are you today?" Candace said to him.

"I'm much better now that you're here. You know you're gentle with the needle, not like those others. I don't think they like me." He looked Candace up and down and then gave her a wink.

"Mr. Hawkins, there will be times when I'm not available and we want you to get the care you need, so today Christine will draw your blood and I'll be here to assist her. Okay Mr. Hawkins?"

"Well alright if you are going to be here, but I'm not sure she knows what she's doing," he said looking at Christine.

Christine prepared to take Mr. Hawkins blood and Candace gave her a reassuring nod. When she was done, Mr. Hawkins had a grin on his face that said he was pleased. Christine was now on her way to being his favorite technician and Candace was assured this problem was resolved.

Candace was glad it was lunch time so that she could talk to Jessica. They picked up their lunches and met up to find a table in the cafeteria.

"Hey girlfriend! I hope your morning started off better than mine. Callie Ann was riding her broom in search of me this morning," Candace said laughing. Jessica just looked at her and shook her head as she watched her dive into the meatloaf and mashed potatoes while still conversing. "Honey, what's the matter?" Candace asked, between chews.

"I was late for work also and Sergeant Noreen was not happy about having to fill in for me. You know I wouldn't be surprised if she has a uniform at home that she practices in and one morning she'll show up with it on after convincing herself that she has earned the stripes."

They both laughed heartily.

"See you needed a laugh too," Candace remarked.

"Yes I do Candace, but to get over my issues I'm going to need more than an occasional laugh."

"Just hold on, everything takes time. God is always working; I know because he's still working on me."

"Oh Holy Mama, don't give me that. By now you and Jesus should be pretty tight."

Candace wanted to tell Jessica just how wrong she really was, but now was not the time.

"Believe me, I'm still a work in progress."

"What do you mean? Candace what were you up to last night? Why were you late this morning?"

"Oh girl, you know I just hate Monday; especially early in the morning."

"Um huh, I also know you're their best technician, but it doesn't make you indispensable."

"Yes, I know. That's why I'm going to be walking the straight and narrow from now on. I don't have any connections in Human Resources anymore."

"Especially after you went to last year's company Halloween party dressed as Mr. Robinson, the Human Resource Director. I still can't believe you did that," Jessica laughed out loud. The people sitting around them were starting to stare. A few of them were well known for carrying the office gossip.

"I guess we should tone it down a bit before somebody wants to join our club, Candace said. "But you have to agree that Mr. Robinson has all of the characteristics of Bozo dressed up in a suit."

"Candace, I think you missed your calling. You should have been a comedian."

"By the way, have you heard from Keith anymore?" she said lowering her voice.

"Oh yes," Jessica replied. "He called again last night. I hung up on him in the middle of him pleading for forgiveness and trying to convince me that his wife is going to give him a divorce."

"Well?" Candace said.

"No Candace. Absolutely not; it's over. I'm depending on you to help me get through this."

"You know I'm here for you girl. Don't forget you can go to God too."

"I'm just not sure God hears my prayers, but I'll keep asking. I don't have anything to lose."

CHAPTER FIVE

"King is his name, but a king he is not." Candace's words still rang in his ears. Nobody knows the truth of that statement better than King himself. He knew that God had changed him, even though he still had some issues that he struggled with.

It was a major step for him when he moved to Chicago twelve years ago. He didn't know anyone and certainly had no intensions of ending up at Mercy Seat. He needed a fresh start and Chicago was comparable to the lifestyle in which he was accustomed to in St. Louis, and big enough to find new job opportunities. He had been on the St. Louis police force for ten years when he made detective. That role was short lived when he was caught in the cross fire of two rival gang members. The doctors were not very optimistic about his survival since the bullet was lodged very close to his heart. No one thought he would survive, including the doctors. After three months in the hospital and six weeks in rehabilitation, he came home to find a disgruntled wife who wanted a divorce. He knew she was unhappy with their marriage because he was guilty of being an unfaithful husband; but he couldn't believe that he had missed the signs of this relationship between his wife and best friend unfolding right under his nose.

George had been his best buddy since they were freshmen in high school. They were inseparable, even spending weekends at each other's homes and calling each of their mothers Mama. George married right after he graduated from high school to do the right thing by his pregnant girlfriend Mia. After two years, they separated, but he took care of George, Jr. just like his mother always taught him to do. "You didn't have your father to take care of you," she would say to George, "so don't do that to your son."

George always wanted to go back to school to become a pharmacist, so he enrolled at the first opportunity. Between work, homework and the baby, he had very little social time. He hung with King when he was still home with his mother and continued when King moved to his own apartment.

When King married Evelyn, she and George hit it off right away, and he continued his Sunday dinner visits with King, especially during football season. Evelyn was a short, very pretty, petite and shapely lady with dark curly hair. She actually encouraged King to have George over, since he lived along.

King had always been a ladies man, even in high school, but when he met Evelyn, he vowed he would be faithful. Although he tried, he found himself straying away and causing much chaos in his marriage. George encouraged him to change his old habits, but when King made detective with the police force, his duties kept him away from home frequently and for long hours. George continued his regular visits on Sunday, even when King was not home. Evelyn was a good cook and King would occasionally find him there watching the game and having dinner. He never suspected any foul play. Perhaps he was too focused on work and his own outside activities to see the signs.

Mercy Seat had been just what he needed according to his mother. She had been persistent in encouraging him to find a church to attend. She had been trying all of his adult life to get him to attend church, but he was having too much fun and he was sure that God wouldn't approve. He wasn't ready to change his lifestyle. Even when he was back on his feet, church was not on his agenda.

One night as he sat in a neighborhood bar a few blocks from home, he heard a voice say "I have allowed you to live to fulfill my purpose for your life. You must use the gifts I have given you." He looked around to see who was speaking. The bartender was at the other end of the bar and no one else was close by.

Later that night as he prepared for bed, he heard that same voice say, "I am everywhere you are. Do my will. I am God and there is no other." It wasn't audible and he couldn't see him, but he heard it just as if he was right in the room with him. He had heard about people hearing the voice of God, but why would God want to talk to him? He spent most of the night thinking about what to do. Maybe he could tell God he wasn't interested.

But he didn't know how to tell God no. He remembered the words of wisdom from his mother. "My son," she said, "When God speaks, listen. When he tells you to do something, obey. When he tells you he's God, believe Him."

His mother was a wise woman, but he still wasn't ready to change his lifestyle. After a few sleepless nights, he decided to at least try. He pulled out the phone book one day and picked out Mercy Seat Church. He liked the name and after several visits he liked the church, so he stayed.

CHAPTER SIX

"Mrs. Clarice Anderson, please stand," Reverend Anderson said. "Now will you all join me in wishing my beautiful wife a happy birthday?" The entire congregation sang happy birthday.

"Thank you, thank you all," she said, smiling and nodding her head that was covered with a wide brim green hat with a satin ribbon.

"Mrs. Anderson, please show the congregation your birthday present." She held up her left hand displaying a beautiful three carat diamond wedding ring. "She's been a wonderful wife. Now she has the ring that I couldn't afford to buy her when we married and I'm taking her on the honeymoon that she has always wanted. Honey, pack your bags and your bikini, I mean your swim suit," he laughed. "We're going to Hawaii for ten days." The entire congregation laughed and applauded.

Jessica could feel someone staring at her. She discreetly turned her head and looked right into the eyes of Mr. Smelling Good, the guy she encountered on her first visit to Mercy Seat.

Wow, she thought. *He looks even better than he did the first time I saw him and he's not sitting with anyone.*

She could tell he was alone because he kept moving his leg in order to keep the little girl sitting next to him from placing her feet on him.

Reverend Anderson began his sermon. "My subject today is *Obedience is What God Wants Most*. If Jesus had to be obedient to his Father, do you think God expects any less from you?"

He said a lot that Jessica didn't understand. She had many thoughts running through her mind.

Jesus and God, aren't they the same? Why is he talking like they are two different people?

It was as if Reverend Anderson had heard her thoughts because at the end of his sermon he announced that he would be teaching a Bible class on the Father, Son and the Holy Spirit. Jessica made a note on her pocket calendar so she would remember to attend. When she was leaving the church, she smelled that familiar fragrance.

"Praise the Lord. It's good to see you again," Jehu said, as he caught up to her.

"It's good to see you also," Jessica said.

"Have a blessed week and do join us again," he said, walking ahead of her.

Reverend Anderson stood at the door shaking hands as the people left the church.

"I hope you were blessed today," he said to Jessica. "Please come back Wednesday night for Bible class."

"I will," Jessica said. "It sounds like it's going to be quite interesting." She hurried to the parking lot to wait for Candace; pacing the pavement impatiently until she saw her coming.

"Candace," she spoke with excitement. "Who is the good looking brother with the nice smile that was sitting in the section to the right side of me? You know the one—"

"Yea, yea, I know who you mean," Candace answered. "That's Jehu."

Jehu – now I have a name for Mr. Smelling Good, she thought.

"Is there something wrong with Jehu or is this someone you're interested in? You've never mentioned him."

"You have to take a ticket and get in line for him and from what I hear the line moves pretty fast."

"What do you mean by that Candace?"

"The word is that the brother can't keep a woman and no one knows why, or at least no one will say why. I'd hate to see you get involved in that scene. You have enough to overcome. Come on let's go eat, I'm hungry."

"Okay, but can we try a new place. I have an appetite for something different," Jessica said, walking toward her car. She stopped abruptly when she realized that Candace was headed for her car also. "Are we taking both cars or is this your way of telling me that my request is denied?"

"Sunday is the only day that I eat fried chicken," Candace said, pausing briefly to get her keys from her purse. "Let's try a new place next Sunday. Okay girlfriend?"

"You never want to compromise Candace. Right now I'm feeling a little put out with you. Do things always have to be—"

Before she could finish, Candace started the car, pulled right up to her and gestured for her to get in. Jessica stood there for a few seconds with one hand on her hip, took a deep breath and then got in the car.

"Deserts on me girlfriend," Candace remarked as she turned the corner without yielding.

CHAPTER SEVEN

"Jehu, my man. How are you?" the voice on the phone asked. "It's been a minute. Are you tired of the church scene yet?"

"Hey Lionel. I'm good and the church scene is just fine."

"Listen man," Lionel continued. "We're planning a bachelor's party for Kevin next Saturday night and I know you don't want to miss it. It's going to be at Sawyer's Banquet Hall."

"You're right, I definitely don't want to miss that party, especially since we have been waiting for ten years for him and Marva to tie the knot," Jehu said, with a bit of sarcasm in his voice.

"Oh, man, ah—he's not marrying Marva. He's marrying Rosalind."

"You mean Rosalind Taylor? You're kidding me."

"I'm sorry Jehu; I just forgot that you and Rosalind had been an item. I didn't mean to be insensitive in breaking the news to you."

"Not a problem. That relationship was done years ago. I'm happy that she found someone, although I never thought it would be Kevin," he said, shaking his head.

"I guess this means that you won't be coming, eh?"

Jehu could hear the disappointment in Lionel's voice. They had been friends since grammar school and Lionel didn't take it too well when he left the club scene for church. He tried to get together with Lionel as much as possible for dinner or an event such as this. He didn't want to lose the friendship or the opportunity to witness to him.

"No sweat man," Jehu assured him. "I'll be there. What time?"

"Nine o'clock. That's the earliest we could convince Kevin to show up. You know his night doesn't start until ten, but we told him that he would lose an hour of fun if he started any later," Lionel said laughing.

"Fine, I'll see you then. It will be good to see everybody," he said trying not to let the shock of the news show in his voice. "Kevin and Rosalind," he spoke aloud, still shocked by the news.

Hearing about Rosalind also made him think about Cynthia, who was his rebound from his breakup with Rosalind. He had really begun to like her and it seemed like the relationship could work until she announced no sex until marriage. He wasn't ready for marriage and definitely not a sexless relationship. After he gave his life to God, he began to understand Cynthia's reasoning, but by then she had moved on to a new relationship.

Being a pharmaceutical sales representative was pretty lucrative, but it came with its own set of challenges. This was a great way to meet women and occasionally he took advantage of the vulnerable women lusting after him. Whether single, married, young or old most of them were looking to fill a void in their lives, and quite often they expected him to be the one to fill it. Since he changed his lifestyle, he had a rule of no dating anyone from the places where he did business. He learned to use the opportunity to do some soul winning.

When he started attending Mercy Seat, he found that the women there were similar to those he encountered outside the church; although he concluded that some of those outside the church weren't quite as desperate and handled rejection much better. Now that he had taken the leadership role over the Singles Ministry, he really had to watch his step.

CHAPTER EIGHT

"No! No! Stop! Don't touch me!" Jessica awakened to a wet pillow and the frightening thoughts that had plagued her mind since she was a young girl. It had been a while since she'd had this dream and she had hoped they were gone forever. Getting over Keith was going to take some time, but the memory of her grandmother's house and all the things that happened to her were engraved in her mind. No matter how she tried to forget, it was all as clear as if it just happened yesterday. She could still hear the creaking of the floor late at night as the footsteps came toward her bedroom door. The scent of the cigar and the sweat from her step grandfather's huge body was still fresh in her nostrils.

She went to live with her grandmother when she was ten after her parents were killed in a car accident. This was a very scary time in Jessica's life to move into a totally different environment with people who, although related, were virtually strangers to her. Her step grandfather was a big man over two hundred pounds, about six feet, three inches tall and his belly hung over the waist of his pants. Although he was well dressed, the neighborhood children called him the Boogie Man because he had huge lips and wore thick glasses. He didn't say much to Jessica, but the way he gawked at her made her very uncomfortable.

Her grandmother was a dark skinned, tall, thin, frail looking lady that wore her gray hair pulled back in a bon. Her clothes were always outdated and she never wore makeup or had her hair done. She seldom laughed, always displaying a distraught look and occasionally a painted smile on her face.

Not long after she arrived, Jessica began to notice her step grandfather constantly watching her every moved. She soon learned to make sure the bathroom door was locked or he would walk in pretending he wasn't aware she was in there. He began luring her to the store with the promise of treating her to candy and ice cream. Once they were in the car, his free hand would roam over her immature body as he told her how much he loved her and how beautiful she was. In the beginning she was not sure what his aim was, but she knew it felt wrong and she was afraid. When she would refuse his invitations to go to the store, her grandmother would insist she go to get out of the house. It was as if she knew what was going on and was promoting his actions. Once Jessica tried to tell her about what he was doing and she told her he was just being affectionate and turned away.

Jessica had no memory of her step grandfather showing any affection toward her grandmother; but when they went to church he was very generous with hugs and kisses with some of the female members who addressed them as Deacon and Mother Atkins. Once she heard her grandmother sobbing as he hit her while telling her to be quiet. He was careful not to leave bruises that could be seen.

For five years Jessica endured this abuse while her grandmother turned a deaf ear and acted as if she was oblivious to what was happening. As the years went by, it all became clear to her why her mother's relationship with her grandmother was estranged and she left home at a young age. They seldom visited her grandmother and when they did her step grandfather never had any conversation with them and would often leave the house. Jessica was never allowed to spend the night, although she thought it was because they lived so far away.

When her grandmother passed away, she moved out of the house, but took with her the horrific memory of her time spent there. The rest of her high school years were spent with a cousin who had a son that she had to constantly distance herself from.

She had never known what a real relationship with a man should be like. As a young teen she had a mature body with all the curves in the right places. It was always a struggle to get past the jealousy and rejection from the girls at school and on into her adulthood.

She learned early that good looks could get her almost any man she desired, but she soon realized that her body was what they wanted most. Jessica wanted a husband, children, and the house with the fenced in yard. But the men she met just wanted to have fun and moved on when she mentioned commitment.

Jessica turned on the television just for a distraction to find that she had only been asleep a little more than an hour. Sleep was what she really needed, but her mind was roaming to places that she didn't want to be. "I'll call Candace," she spoke aloud. "Talking to her will pull me back into reality." She dialed her number.

"Hi, this is Candace. I can't talk right now. At the beep, leave your name and number and we'll chat later."

"Candace, girl where are you when I need you? Call me." She had barely hung up, when the phone rang again. Jessica answered quickly. "Candace, where have you been?"

"Jessica, please don't hang up. Just give me five minutes, please."

She hesitated before speaking. "Okay Keith, but you only get three minutes starting right now."

"Honey I admit that I started out deceiving you and I know I hurt you. But please believe me; I fell in love with you. That is the real truth, so help me God. I have been a lousy husband, but I love my children and I'm a good father. My wife has asked me for a divorce and I have consented. If you have a change of heart, call me. I want to work things out for us. I'm not giving you up this easy. I love you Jessica." He hung up.

Jessica just wanted closure and the constant calls from Keith kept the wounds of her aching heart open. She had to end it once and for all.

CHAPTER NINE

A short busty lady with big hips and dark red hair pushed a man in a wheel chair down the aisle to the front of the church and put the safety latch on his chair. Jessica had seen them before from afar. He was a tall, handsome and well-dressed man. From his wheelchair he enjoyed watching the ladies as he rolled by.

"That's Millie and Deacon Daniel McKay," Candace whispered to Jessica. "She's over the teaching ministry."

King Jordan acknowledged Jessica with a nod of his head as he sat down across the aisle. Candace looked straight ahead as if she didn't see him. Suddenly that familiar fragrance got Jessica's attention. She didn't need to turn around to know that it was Jehu behind her.

Jessica's curiosity and Candace's coaxing had convinced her to come to Bible study. Her eyes surveyed the walls of the church. The evening sun shining through the stained glass windows reflected on the wooden cross with Jesus nailed to it.

He looks so helpless. Could this possibly be the Jesus I came to learn about and want to meet?

She snickered softly as she tried to imagine Jesus standing up for her.

"What's funny?" Candace asked.

"Oh, just a funny thought crossed my mind," she replied smiling. She really wanted to understand more about Jesus, God and the Holy Spirit. Jesus hanging on the cross is not how she visualized him at all. She couldn't imagine anyone giving their life for her, especially Jesus. Reverend Anderson began teaching and Jessica opened her Bible and prepared to take notes. She focused all of her attention on what he was saying.

"Jesus on the cross is just a reminder of what he did for each of us; the sacrifice he made so that we might have eternal life. Jesus is alive and powerful. His name alone causes demons to tremble because even they know who he is," Reverend Anderson shouted.

Jessica couldn't understand how people could believe in and worship a being they could not see. It was beyond her comprehension how you could get to know God and have a relationship with him by reading and studying the Bible. Reverend Anderson made it all sound so real and believable. Right now this Jesus that she was trying to understand might be her only hope.

When they were leaving the church, Candace introduced her to Reverend Ben, an assistant minister in the church.

"I'm so pleased to meet you Jessica and glad you came to Bible class," Reverend Ben said.

"Thank you, Reverend Ben. It's certainly been interesting," Jessica replied.

"You will come again, won't you?"

"Yes, I think I will," Jessica said. As they were exiting the church, Jessica smelled that fragrance again.

"Sister Candace, how are you?" the voice behind them said.

"I'm doing fine Jehu," she said, turning around to acknowledge him and then quickly turning to proceed to the car.

"Hello, I'm Jehu Edwards," he said to Jessica, reaching out to shake her hand.

"I'm Jessica Jones," she said smiling as her hand met his.

What a smile and beautiful light brown eyes. I wonder if they are his or contacts. It doesn't matter. He looks better each time I see him.

"Jessica, I noticed you have been here a few times. If you decide to join our family here at Mercy Seat, please consider the singles ministry. Pardon me, I should have asked if you're single?"

"I am single and I'll keep that in mind." Jessica smiled.

"I'll fill her in Jehu," Candace yelled back as she hurried to her car.

"Thanks again for the invitation Jehu." Jessica's heart raced as she walked away. She couldn't believe that he was stirring up her feelings like that. Her heart was in desperate need of healing right now. Maybe it was just her imagination, she thought.

"Candace, why are you in such a hurry? You were rude to Jehu for no reason."

"I told you Jessica, Jehu's reputation is shaky. I'm praying for you to get over Keith. Do you really need more drama in your life right now?"

"I appreciate you standing guard over my life, but allow me to make my own decisions. I am an adult you know."

"Okay Jessica, but I'm warning you, beware of wolves in sheep's clothes. I'll see you at work tomorrow," she said, as her heels clicked the sidewalk rapidly.

Jessica didn't like being left in the middle of a conversation. Even though she was upset with Candace, she was still grateful that she was concerned about her. On the way home she pulled into the parking lot of the supermarket. Inside the store she searched through her purse for her list and pulled a cart out to shop.

"Let me get that for you," a man said, as she reached to the top shelf for her favorite cereal. Candace turned to say thanks and was surprised to see King.

"Hello Mr. King. How are you?"

"I'm blessed Jessica, how about you? He placed the cereal in her cart. "Can I reach something else for you?" he said, taking control of the cart.

"I just need water and I'm done."

"Great, I'll push the cart for you."

"Didn't you stop for something?" she asked.

"I need water also. I can just put it in your cart."

Jessica could feel his eyes roaming up and down her body. Candace was right, she thought. You know he's checking you out even with the dark glasses on.

"I'm happy to see you attending Bible class. That shows your sincerity in seeking a relationship with God," King remarked.

"Do you live in the neighborhood Mr. Jordan? I mean King," she said smiling.

"No I just stop here because it's on the way home from church and convenient. How about stopping for coffee before you head home? It will give me an opportunity to talk to you about Mercy Seat. You must have a lot of questions."

Is he being honest or is this another come on line?

"Oh come on, if you're afraid the caffeine will keep you up, just have some decaf or some juice."

Although she felt skeptical about his motives, she thought it would be safe to just have coffee with him. After all, she was tired of going home alone and he wasn't a total stranger.

"Alright, just one cup of coffee and I have to head home. I have an early morning."

"I promise you'll be home by ten."

They checked out and headed for the coffee shop across the street. Jessica decided on an herbal tea. She didn't need anything else to keep her awake. King ordered coffee and they sat down at a table by the window.

"Jessica, where did you worship before you came to Mercy Seat?" He poured a lot of cream into his coffee as he talked.

"Oh, ah—I didn't go to church. I guess I'm what you Christians call a heathen," she said, laughing and putting sugar in her tea.

"I would never call you a heathen; however, I am glad you decided to seek the Lord. Most of all I'm glad you came to Mercy Seat," he said, sipping his coffee.

Jessica poured more sugar in her tea and squeezed fresh lemon, careful not to squirt it. She hoped he wouldn't ask any more questions that she didn't want to answer.

"How do you like Mercy Seat so far?"

"I like the messages I'm hearing. I'm curious to know more about Jesus. I keep hearing marvelous things about him and how he worked miracles. Why isn't he depicted as a strong, robust superman? How can I believe in someone that is portrayed as a weakling?"

"You have great questions and I promise you that if you keep coming to church and Bible classes, you'll get your answers and you won't be disappointed. Besides being our Lord and Savior, he is so much more to us. In time you will be able to decide who you want him to be in your life."

"How do I really get to know him? Will he come and introduce himself to me?" Jessica asked curiously.

King laughed as he excused himself to go to his car. He returned with a package wrapped in pretty blue paper. "Here is something that will help you get to know Jesus," he said handing her the package.

She could tell that it was a book by the shape. She carefully removed the beautiful paper and underneath was a leather-bound burgundy Bible with tabs for each book. Her name was engraved on the cover in gold letters. Inside was a handwritten note that read—

To Jessica,

A woman that God has many blessings for and is gifted to teach his people. Jessica, meet Jesus who will save you and free you from all that holds you captive. Have a blessed journey.

King Jordan

"Thank you King; this is so special. I will treasure it. How did you know I needed a Bible?"

"I saw the one you've been using. It looked a little worn. Please accept it as a welcome gift to Mercy Seat. Start with the book of John and study the chapters that are recommended in Bible class. You'll be fine Jessica. Seek the Lord and he'll meet you where you are."

She was glad that she had stopped with King. Now she had something to help her get better acquainted with God.

CHAPTER TEN

Jessica decided to get involved in some of the church activities. Since Jehu had invited her, she thought the singles ministry would be a good place to start and perhaps meet some new people. There were more women than men and mostly middle aged people. After the meeting Jehu asked her to wait for him to escort her to her car. Jessica noticed that there were not a lot of good choices of men. She was surprised to see King there.

"Jessica, it's always a pleasure. I see you're taking my advice and getting involved."

"Good to see you King," Jessica replied smiling.

"King, I'm glad you came out tonight," Jehu said, as he shook his hand. "I haven't seen you at any singles events for a while."

"Sometimes my busy schedule doesn't permit me to be everywhere I'd like to be. It was worthwhile making the sacrifice tonight to hear Elder Mosby teach on being single and living holy. Singles need to know how to abstain according to the word."

"I agree and he was very encouraging to all of us. I'm looking forward to seeing you at the next event." Jehu reached his arm around Jessica's back guiding her away from King.

Jessica sensed the tension between the two men. She didn't feel comfortable asking, so she tried another approach. "Have you known Mr. King very long?"

"He was a member here at Mercy Seat when I came. He seems to be somewhat of a loner, yet he knows everybody."

Jessica slowed down her pace hoping that she would get an answer before she got to her car. "How do you explain that?"

"I can't explain it. He's on the Board of Directors here at the church you know. I don't know if King is someone that you would want to get to know. He has, for lack of a better word, a strange reputation. Not bad, just strange."

Jessica walked slowly and continued to probe. "What do you mean by strange?"

"Can we discuss this over dinner on Saturday evening? That would give me an opportunity to get to know you better," Jehu said, displaying that wonderful smile that could get a yes from any girl.

Jessica stopped and looked at him. She didn't want to seem desperate. "Are you asking me on a date or is this one of those saints getting together to eat deals?" she asked, blushing.

"This is definitely a request for a dinner date, no strings attached."

"In that case I accept."

They exchanged phone numbers and agreed on a time before she finally made it to her car and said good night.

CHAPTER ELEVEN

Candace was glad church was over. She headed down the corridor to meet Jessica so they could go to Mandy's to eat. She spotted Albert standing along the wall near the exit. There was no way she could get by him without being seen.

"Hello there, sexy mama. I've been missing you," he said in a low voice.

"Ditto my sweet," Candace replied, as she discreetly looked around to see if anyone was close by to hear her.

"Can I get on your schedule this evening?" he said licking his lips and smiling.

"I'm on my way to eat with my friend Jessica. I encouraged her to come to Mercy Seat to work on getting her life straight, so I'm trying to make her feel welcome here. I should be free around five."

"I'll see you later," he said tucking his Bible under his arm and holding the door for Candace to exit.

Candace felt bad about the way she treated Albert. She knew it was wrong to sneak around with him and then act like she barely knew him in front of the church members. She had been seeing Albert for several years and honestly didn't understand why he put up with her nonsense. They spent most of their time together behind closed doors, because she didn't want anyone to know about him until she made up her mind to commit to the relationship. She wasn't sure if that would ever happen. He had bought an engagement ring a year ago and asked her to marry him, but she put him off by saying she needed more time to make sure this was the right time. She knew Albert loved her and she cared a lot for him, but he lacked some of the things that she desired in a man. She wanted someone tall, good looking, and articulate, educated and making six figures. Albert was a good looking guy, but he was only five feet nine and a flamboyant dresser. He loved colorful suits and bold ties. He didn't have a college education, but he had a good job. He was willing to take her to the best places; however, she was ashamed to let everyone know she was having a relationship with him because he was the total opposite of the man of her dreams.

She hurried to catch up with Jessica so they could head to Mandy's. She hoped Jessica hadn't seen her with Albert because she was not ready to share her secret.

She managed to keep the conversation on other things, but when they were at dinner, Jessica started probing again about Albert. Candace tried to ignore her, but it was useless.

"Candace, did you hear me? Were you thinking about the little short cute brother with the loud suit? I saw you talking today and I've seen him giving you the eye before. Is he trying to come on to you?" Jessica asked.

"That's Albert. He's a nice guy, but not my type."

"You could me missing out on a good relationship by not looking at his good qualities. I know he's probably not all you desire in a man, but he's good looking, goes to church and he obviously likes you."

"Like I said, he's not my type," Candace said, biting into a piece of chicken. "I just love fried chicken, don't you Jessica? She closed her eyes and chewed slowly, savoring the chicken.

"Yea, sure"

"What kind of answer is that Jessica?

"Candace, I'm eating fish, so what does that tell you? Jessica answered, taking her fork to separate her baked tilapia.

"Girl, when I'm eating fried chicken with a little hot sauce, it's the next best thing to heaven," Candace laughed.

"Really," Jessica remarked staring into space.

"What's eating you?" Candace asked with her mouth full. "Too many guys hitting on you at Mercy Seat?"

"No, it's not the guys I'm concerned about; it's the females. They aren't very friendly and I sense that I'm the frequent topic of conversation. I get that look as I walk by and even when they speak to me it doesn't seem genuine. This is not what I expected from holy people. Do you know what I mean?" She leaned toward Candace to make sure she was paying attention.

"Yes," Candace said between chews. "I know exactly what you mean. They are just hating on you girlfriend. But you've dealt with that all of your life. You can handle a few jealous women, can't you?" She stopped eating and looked at Jessica. "What is really bothering you?"

"I feel like a misfit. I don't think Jesus is interested in someone like me. How can I ask Jesus, the almighty to do anything for me? I've lived such an awful life style."

"Listen to me Jessica Jones," Candace interrupted. "You're just a human being that's searching for something that only God can give you. There are no perfect people Jessica, they just wish they were. Almost everyone at Mercy Seat has an unscrupulous past. They all came to God with their bags of mess, including me."

"Not you holy Mama. You were always on the straight and narrow path."

Candace wanted to make sure Jessica believed what she was saying. She reached over and touched her hand to get her undivided attention. "Yes Jessica, me too. When God gave his son as a sacrifice, he did it for whosoever would believe in Jesus Christ. I'm just a member of the Whosoever Will Club and you can be a member too. Now quit having a pity party. If it will make you feel better, our own Deacon Wills used to be a drug dealer. You know sweet lovable Deacon Wills?"

"You're kidding. No way," Jessica said laughing.

"Back in the day, the brother had a business without a license. But that was many years ago. See what God has done for him. He can change you too if you allow him. Now let me get back to my food. You know I hate cold food," she said, quickly wiping the tear running down her face. "While I'm having dessert, I'll tell you about Reverend Ben."

"Oh, don't tell me he was a pimp or something," Jessica said, shaking her head.

Candace laughed and spewed her soda out on the table. "No Jessica, no way," Candace whispered. She was blushing. "I think I'm falling for Reverend Ben."

"Really! You never let on. Why?"

"I wasn't sure how I felt, but lately he's been acting interested in me and it's gotten my attention. You know the extra long hand holding when he greets me. And the way he says Sister Candace just puts the icing on the cake."

"Has he asked you out yet?"

"No, but I expect him to soon. I think he has so many women pulling at him until he's just trying to be cautious. Now that I know he's interested, I'll walk a little slower when he's in view, she said smiling, as she reached for the hot apple cobbler and ice cream that the waitress placed on the table.

"You're not the only one that has some news hot off the press," Jessica said.

"I'm listening." Candace was eager to hear this news.

"I have a date with Mr. Smelling Good." She smiled and waited for approval from Candace.

"I guess you want to test the waters for yourself, eh? I told you Jessica, his reputation precedes him. He's –"

"Hold on Candace. It's just dinner. It will give me a chance to get to know him for myself. It's not like he's a suspected serial killer or something, so just calm down."

"Alright," Candace said raising both hands. "Don't say I didn't warn you."

"It would be nice if you would just tell me what you know about him."

"Rumor has it that he's a womanizer. The women that he has dated at Mercy Seat won't really talk about him after it's all over. Something is seriously wrong. Maybe you can find out since you're so determined to date him," Candace said, folding her arms and sighing.

"All I know is that the brother is fine, intelligent, saved and has a job. Even outside the church those are good qualities in a man. And let's not forget that he smells good." They both laughed.

"Girlfriend, I'm glad you have a sense of humor, even though it's sometimes a little warped," Candace said, shoving more cobbler and ice cream into her mouth.

CHAPTER TWELVE

Jessica took a look at herself from head to toe in the mirror. She had changed three times and the little black dress seemed to have won out. It was square at the chest with off the shoulder straps. The hemline was fashionably short, a few inches above the knees; simple but sexy. The doorbell rang helping her to make up her mind about the dress. The minute she laid eyes on him, her heart began to flutter. She took a deep breath and placed her hand over her heart as she closed the door behind him.

"Jessica, you look absolutely ravishing," he said, giving her a kiss on the cheek. She smelled that fragrance that she loved so much.

It must be my imagination that this guy gets finer every time I see him.

He wore a black Lycra cotton shirt, black plain front tapered straight leg slacks with a black and white Houndstooth blazer and black Cohan loafers.

"You look great too Jehu," she said blushing. "Come in for a moment while I grab a wrap, just in case it gets cool in the restaurant."

"That's fine," he said closing the door, "but I have two arms and a jacket in case you need it.

"It's a very nice jacket and I'll keep that in mind," she said, taking a shawl from the closet.

He gently placed his hand around her waist as he opened the door for her to exit.

The ambiance of the restaurant was great, just as she remembered it when Keith would bring her here. When Jehu told her where they were going, she couldn't let on just how familiar she was with Jessup's Steak House. She simply said it had great food. Keith would always say they were going to her restaurant. When the waitress came, she had already decided to order her usual.

"I'll have the prime rib, medium well, the twice baked potato, and a small salad with blue cheese dressing," she told the waitress.

"You must be a mind reader Jessica." Jehu looked at her and then to the waitress. I'll have the same with ranch dressing and please make sure the bread is warm."

"Of course sir, I'll be right back with your champagne."

"How did she know you wanted champagne? You didn't order it. Is she psychic?"

"I suppose that she could tell by my guest that I wanted the best."

"In that case, she made a good assumption."

"Actually I made the request for champagne when I made the reservations."

Now she understood why the waiter always brought champagne to the table when she had dinner with Keith without him asking for it.

"Thanks for being honest with me." Jessica picked up her glass of water from the table and took a sip.

"He excused himself from the table and shortly afterwards a different waitress appeared and handed Jessica a note. She quickly opened the note and read it.

Jessica, I didn't want to interrupt your evening, but I couldn't pass up the opportunity to say hello. You look happy and beautiful as always. Please let me see you later. I'm flying out in the morning. Keith

She looked around in three different directions before she spotted Keith lifting his glass to her. The two men sitting with him looked on with a smile of approval.

"Thank you," Jessica said to the waitress.

"The gentlemen asked me to wait for a response."

"Tell him—tell him to have a safe trip home." She crumpled the note up in her hand and Jehu returned just as the waitress was walking away.

"Jessica, did we get a new waitress while I was gone? Is there a problem?" he said after Jessica didn't respond.

"Nothing that matters," she said managing a smile.

"It does matter. I don't want anything or anybody to ruin our evening. Now tell me what happened. I want to clear this up before we get to my favorite part of the evening." He could tell by the look on Jessica's face that he needed to clarify that statement expeditiously. "Dessert is my favorite part of dinner. You do like dessert, don't you?" he said gently touching her hand.

"Yes, of course I do. It's my favorite part of dinner as well." She opened her hand and revealed the crumpled piece of paper for Jehu to read. He read it and looked at her for a response.

"It's from an ex-boyfriend with no chance of reconciliation. I told the waitress to tell him to have a good trip home."

Jehu sat back in his chair and picked up the menu. "Let's look at the dessert menu. The turtle cheesecake is my favorite. What looks good to you?"

Right now nothing looks better than you; absolutely nothing, she thought.

"It's one of my favorite too," she said, looking at him instead of the menu.

As the evening continued, they laughed and talked as if they had been acquainted for years. Besides having a great sense of humor, Jehu was a good conversationalist. Jessica liked those qualities in a man. She felt safe and comfortable with him. They discovered they had more in common than their choice of food and drink. Neither of them had ever been married, had no children, loved music, and liked to read.

This man is too good to be true. He has such great qualities all wrapped in a good looking package. A sister could really get attached to this brother.

Jessica was enjoying the evening so much until she didn't want it to end. She wondered just how it was going to end. Would all of his perfect manners disappear and like all the others, begin to hint around to getting an invitation to her apartment; or try to convince her to go home with him?

He held her hand as they stood at her apartment door. "Jessica, thank you for a wonderful evening and great conversation. I hope we can do this again soon."

"I hope so too." She anticipated that this would be the best part of the evening. She waited for him to seal the night with that kiss that she had been waiting for.

"Good night," he said, planting a kiss on her cheek.

"Good night Jehu."

Well this evening certainly didn't end like I planned, nor then it end like all the others.

The message light on Jessica's phone was lit. She checked the caller ID. It was from Candace.

"Jessica, hurry up and call me. I want to know all the details of the evening."

There was a second message and Jessica hoped that it wasn't Keith. It was Candace again.

"Jessica, what's taking you so long?"

The light was still lit and she listened.

"Jessica, I'm sorry. I didn't mean to spoil your evening, but it was good to see you. I hope to see you again, under different circumstances of course. Please call me. Please."

A message from Keith was just what she didn't want or need. She had barely hung up the phone when it rang again. She checked the caller ID before answering.

"Girl, why are you making me sweat?"

"Calm down Candace. I've only been home long enough to get your messages. The dinner was great right up to dessert. The conversation was marvelous and he is still fine and smelling good," Jessica said laughing as she spoke fast mimicking Candace. Candace joined her in the laughter.

"We had one small interruption."

"What? Who?"

"Keith in the flesh."

"You have got to be kidding. What did he say to Jehu?"

"Nothing, he was nice enough to send a note to the table while Jehu was away." Jessica gave Candace the details.

"So is there a happy ending to this evening?"

"Absolutely, he wants to see me again."

"Did he try to—?"

"No Candace. He was a perfect gentleman all night. He gave me a kiss on the cheek and said good night at the door."

"Well I'm taking notes. I'm going to find out the mystery behind Mr. Jehu."

CHAPTER THIRTEEN

Jessica was learning a lot from Reverend Anderson's Bible classes in the few months that she had been attending Mercy Seat. She was seriously thinking about becoming a member, but she hadn't planned to do it today. Her body just seemed to lift itself from the bench and her wobbly legs moved her down the aisle to answer the alter call to accept Jesus into her life and get baptized. Candace walked beside her encouraging her and holding her arm.

"Candace," Jessica whispered. "I'm not sure I'm ready for this. My legs are shaking and my heart is beating so fast that I think I'm going to have a heart attack."

"Don't worry Jessica, just lean on me. We're not going to let a little heart pounding and nerves keep you from getting saved from hell and damnation. You stood up and started to the altar by yourself. God is drawing you and I'm just here to encourage you," she said keeping a tight grip on Jessica's arm. "See, you're here." She stepped back leaving Jessica to stand on her own.

Getting baptized was more than just getting immersed into a pool of water. Jessica felt renewed and refreshed. Something happened that she couldn't explain. She heard a voice say, "I am God and there is no other." She waited for more conversation but there was none. After the baptism, she dressed and went to meet Candace.

"Now I'm assured that we will always be together, even in heaven," Candace said embracing Jessica.

Jessica tried to explain to Candace how she was feeling and what happened, but she couldn't find the words to describe her experience. It was something that she had never experienced before and she felt happy.

"I know Jessica, it's wonderful," Candace kept saying.

Reverend and First Lady Anderson stood by to welcome all of the new converts. "Welcome to Mercy Seat," Reverend Anderson said, as he shook Jessica's hand.

First Lady Anderson gave Jessica a welcome hug. "Jessica, we're so glad you made the right choice to let Jesus in your life. My office door is always open to you if you have questions or desire any counseling."

"Thank you First Lady Anderson. I have plenty of questions, so keep that door wide opened," Jessica said laughing.

"We have several ministries for young women like you. After you complete the new member's classes, please review the ministry packets and give some thought to where you might want to get involved. Meanwhile continue to attend Bible classes." She quickly turned her attention to the lady pushing the man in the wheelchair. "Oh Sister Millie, she called. "I want you to meet Jessica Jones. She has just been baptized. Jessica, meet Millie and Daniel McKay."

"I'm pleased to meet you Mr. & Mrs. McKay."

"Sister Millie is in charge of the teaching ministry," First Lady Anderson said. "Millie, I'd like for you to mentor Jessica if she decides on the teaching ministry."

"It would be my pleasure Jessica. I will be at the last two new members sessions explaining about the training program for aspiring teachers. We are so in need of more good teachers, so I hope you will consider it."

"I once wanted to be a teacher, but I never continued school for my degree. Would that be a challenge if I decide to teach here at the church?" Jessica asked.

"Oh, no Jessica. We just need to determine if this is the right ministry for you. We do require that you know the Word of God and take the training classes here at the church," Millie explained.

"I will certainly give it some consideration as I go through the new members training. I'll let you know Sister Millie."

"I look forward to hearing from you Jessica."

Deacon McKay was watching Jessica as she and Millie conversed. Finally he spoke. "Congratulations Jessica. I know God will point you in the right direction."

"Thank you Mr. McKay."

Millie had seen that look in his eyes many times before, but it was for her. She whirled his chair around and hurriedly pushed him out of the sanctuary.

Candace and Jessica looked at each other and then at Millie and Daniel as they existed the church. Jessica couldn't understand why Millie seemed upset at Daniel welcoming her into the church.

"Let's go. I think you've had enough introductions for now. You'll get to know Mean Millie and Flirty Dan soon enough," Candace said, as they walked to their cars.

"You mean Sister Millie?"

"No, I mean what I said. Don't let that phony smile fool you. And don't have too much conversation with Deacon McKay. He still flirts from his wheelchair and she still acts as if someone actually wants him. Let's go celebrate. All this excitement is making me hungry."

"You don't need an excuse to eat, but this time I'm choosing the place. You can skip fried chicken today. We're going where we can have seafood or steak. Okay?"

"I guess," Candace said reluctantly.

"Fantastic! I'm driving and you can pay," Jessica said laughing. "By the way, I see the little short brother with the loud suits is on your trail again and you were actually having a conversation with him."

"Albert is quite persistent. No matter what I say, he just won't give up. He's nice, but like I told you before, he's not my type."

"Just how long has he been persistent? Maybe you should at least go out with him; have some real conversation and find out some things about him."

"You really think I should go out with him?"

"Yes, I would at least have dinner. If nothing else you might become good friends. He might find out that he doesn't like you as much as he thinks he does; or you might like him more than you think you do. You know men are so visual, but you can't blame the brother for pursuing you."

Candace didn't want to discuss Albert with Jessica. It was enough that she felt guilty about her relationship with him. She really needed to make a decision about Albert. God was certainly not pleased with their actions behind closed doors and she was tired of asking for forgiveness. "Jessica, if it will get you off my back, I'll go out with him and check him out."

"Great, but don't try right away to wrestle him out of those loud suits, you might have a fight on your hands."

They both laughed. Candace knew Jessica was speaking the truth.

CHAPTER FOURTEEN

Daniel tried to cut the skin from the chicken without Millie noticing, but as usual she was watching every move he made, even at the dinner table.

"Why don't you say it? Say it Daniel!" Millie's voice went from low to a high pitch.

"Say what Millie?" Daniel responded calmly. His calmness only intensified her anger.

"Why did you fry my chicken Millie? You know I have to watch my cholesterol," she mimicked him. "Well dam your cholesterol and you too."

"What is it this time Millie? Nobody complimented you on your new outfit at church today?"

"Not being able to walk certainly doesn't hinder your eyes from roaming. I saw that Miss Jessica smiling and flirting with you. When I'm finished with her she will regret she ever set foot in Mercy Seat."

"When are you going to stop blaming everybody else for your problems Millie? You can't get your youth back and start all over again, but you can get delivered from those spirits of rejection, jealousy and hatred and a few of their cousins. Millie you have become a whole different person from when I met you. You were vibrant, humorous and searching for a new life when we met. Now the people at church call you Mean Millie behind your back. That painted smile you wear and those cute little sarcastic compliments you throw out aren't fooling anyone. Millie I still love you and always have. Let go and allow God to heal you. Get some counseling. I'll come with you and—"

Millie banged her fork on the table, stood up and put both hands on the table as she leaned over to get closer to Daniel. "Don't you dare talk to me about love! Were you telling Miss Thang how much you love me when your car plowed into that laundromat? It's a good thing it was closed and nobody was killed. Your slutty passenger walked away and here you are wheeling around in your chair. Tell me Daniel, do you still think God is going to heal you?" She looked at him with a smirk on her face as she sat down.

Daniel was handsome and once considered a real Casanova. He owned a real estate business that was very lucrative for him. When he married Millie, she was beautiful, but that beauty was now covered up by excess weight, make-up, bitterness and anger. Five years into their marriage Daniel was in a car accident that left him paralyzed and legally blind in one eye, although some say that at the right moment he has 20/20 vision. The woman that was in the car with him only sustained a broken arm and a fractured ankle. In the prime of her life Millie was left with an invalid husband and she hated having to care for him; but Daniel had invested his money well and she wasn't about to let anyone else share in the wealth. He believed that God would heal him, but as the years went by Millie constantly reminded him that he was still confined to his wheelchair.

Millie retreated to the bedroom and shut the door. She intended to lie on the bed, but landed on her knees and cried uncontrollably. "Why do I hurt people that love me and that I love? Why do I want to destroy people that have done nothing to hurt me? Why Lord?" she said, between sobs. "Why have you left me in this place? I was willing to follow you. Help me!"

"When you stopped focusing on me, you lost your way." Millie knew that voice. It had directed and comforted her many times. It was the same voice that told her he would give her a new life if she would commit her life to him. There was no doubt in her mind that it was the Spirit of the Lord. She couldn't believe that she had allowed herself to get to this place of doubt and bitterness. She remembered where God had brought her from. It was a place that she never wanted to be again.

CHAPTER FIFTEEN

Jessica was looking Candace up and down trying to figure out why she looked more like she was going to a nightclub than to church.

"Girl, aren't we going to church this morning. Did you change your mind?"

"Oh no, I am definitely going to church. Reverend Ben is preaching today and this is my opportunity to get his attention."

"Aren't you ushering today?"

"No, today is my Sunday off. I can sit in the audience and be face to face with Reverend Ben when he speaks. You know it's been a few years since his wife died and there are no rumors of him having any real commitment to anyone. Well there's Serita Noble in the choir. You know the one who is anointed to scream and give everybody a headache." They both laughed loudly as Candace continued to admire herself in the mirror.

"He's been seen talking to her, but it didn't look like more than a casual conversation," Candace continued.

"You mean the one with the three dimensional hairdo and she walks like she has a rod in her back?"

"Yes, that's the one."

Jessica continued describing her. "And when you speak to her she gives you a smirk instead of speaking back?"

"Yes, that's Serita," Candace agreed. "She has money and is one of the trustees of the church. She drives a Lexus and gets a new one every two years. She was eyeballing Reverend Ben before his wife became ill and now that she has passed away, I'm sure she's doing all she can to get his attention."

"Oh yea, she definitely can't sing and she's real related to ugly." Jessica placed one hand on the side of her face and the other on Candace's shoulder. "Okay girlfriend, let's give her some competition, but leave something to the imagination. Right now you're showing too much cleavage. You will have every man looking at you and every woman talking about you. What about the green dress that accents your figure with the V-neck? You always stop traffic in that and I bet you have never worn that to church."

"I don't know. Ah—," Candace stammered with a frown on her face as she tried to ignore Jessica.

"Listen, you invited me to church and now I'm trying to do this thing right. The least you can do is set a good example. If I can lower my hemline surely you can show a little less flesh. The word says when a man finds a wife, he finds a good thing. He won't need to find you with all of your boobs popping out saying here I am, come and get me."

Candace knew Jessica was right, but she wasn't about to let her get away with that. "I know you're not preaching to me," she said placing her hands on her hips and rolling her neck as she talked. "Last Sunday Brother Jehu could hardly pay attention to the message for looking across the aisle at you."

"I did nothing to initiate that."

"Maybe not but the slit up the side of your skirt was saying a whole lot."

"Candace, we're going to be late for church. Will you just put on the dress so we can go?"

Candace hesitantly pulled out the green dress and put it on. She remembered that she always received compliments when she wore this dress and agreed with Jessica that she looked good in it. They hurried out to church with Jessica reassuring her that she had made the right choice.

Candace sat on the right side of the church on the front row to be sure that Reverend Ben could see her. She made sure she had her Bible out, turning to scriptures when he called them out. She shouted loudly whenever the congregation said amen. Jessica elbowed her when she crossed her short shapely legs allowing her dress to slightly expose her thighs. She couldn't believe Candace's behavior; especially in church. When the service was over, Candace rushed to get in the line to say hello to Reverend Ben.

"Sister Candace, it's so good to see you. It's nice that you had today to sit and enjoy the service."

"I truly enjoyed it Reverend Ben. You brought such an inspiring word. I'll have to buy the DVD so I can refresh my memory and study the points you brought out." She placed her free hand on Jessica's shoulder urging her to keep walking, but Reverend Ben let go of her hand and reached over and took Jessica's hand to greet her.

"Sister Jessica, how are you?"

Candace watched his eyes light up.

"I'm doing just fine Reverend Ben."

"I'm glad you decided to join our church family. If you need any help or advice, please feel free to call on me."

"Thank you, I will." Jessica released his hand and moved past him. She walked out with Candace.

"Well next week I'm going shopping."

"What for this time Candace?"

"I need to buy a Reverend Ben dress. This one obviously didn't work. He barely noticed me for looking at you."

Jessica couldn't believe Candace's display of jealousy. She tried to think of something humorous, but she found herself speechless. She had never given much thought to Reverend Ben, but now that she had taken a closer look, she could see why Candace was interested in him. Even under the robe you could tell that he had a nice set of abs. Although he was slightly bald and wore glasses, on a scale of one to ten, he was a definite eight in the looks department.

"Candace I'm sorry that you didn't get the attention from Reverend Ben that you hoped for, but don't you think you went overboard trying? Isn't it his role to come after you? Maybe I'm wrong, but I thought the church did things differently from the world. I know I should be the last person to say these things to you, but it's because of what I have been through in my life that I can."

Candace didn't want to admit that Jessica was right. "Alright Jessica, I hear you loud and clear. Stop preaching at me and let's go eat."

CHAPTER SIXTEEN

The day was going well except for the patients complaining of having to wait too long. Today was Jessica's birthday and normally an exciting day for her, but today no one seemed to remember and she was glad because she didn't have to explain why Keith was not in her life anymore. He usually made sure that everybody knew with his surprise deliveries.

"Henry North Hospital outpatient registration, Jessica speaking. How may I help you?"

"Miss Jones, you have a delivery at the security desk."

"I'm not expecting anything. What is it?"

"It's wrapped up and a signature is needed," Clyde the security guard said, smacking his chewing gum. "Oh, and the delivery guy says he's double parked."

"I'll be right there."

She could see his tall slender body as she got near the security desk. It was Keith and she knew it would be the gossip of the week if she didn't greet him. She beckoned for him to come meet her.

"Hello Jessica. This is the only way I could get to see you." He handed her a dozen red roses. "Please accept them and for the sake of all the eyes that are looking at us right now, try to smile and let me give you a kiss."

"Just for the sake of all the eyes Keith, but afterwards you make haste out of here and don't do this again," Jessica said, faking a smile.

He leaned over and kissed her on the cheek and handed her a small miniature hand bag. "Happy birthday baby. I'm in town until tomorrow evening. I hope you will reconsider and call me." He turned and exited the building with a grand smile as if he was the knight who had just found his princess. She watched him walk away knowing that a piece of her heart went with him; then hurried back to her desk to phone Candace.

"Candace, can you meet me for lunch early?"

"I think so, we're not very busy. Are you okay? You sound upset."

"Just meet me. I'll explain then."

"Fine, I'll meet you at 11:45. I won't be able to justify leaving earlier."

"That's fine, but meet me out front. We're not going to the cafeteria. We're going to McDonalds."

"McDonalds! But today is fish, mac and cheese day," Candace said raising her voice.

"I know Candace, but it's also red rose's day," Jessica whispered.

"Oh—okay, meeting you out front," Candace whispered back.

They sat down to eat and Jessica handed the roses to Candace. "These are for you. Enjoy them."

"Are you serious? These are beautiful."

"That's why you should have them because you think they're beautiful. They only remind me of Keith. I wish he would just leave me alone. He's making it very difficult for me to move on with my life," Jessica said picking in her chicken salad.

Candace dove into her fish and fries. "This is no substitute for the real thing." She looked at the face of her friend and realized that Jessica was hurting and she was being insensitive. "I'm sorry Jessica, I'm listening to you. Actually the fries are good and hot and the fish is pretty tasty," she said filling her mouth with a handful of fries. "What's in the bag? Is that for me too?"

"This is the surprise after the surprise," Jessica remarked.

"Well, let's open it. Come on, do you want me to do it?" Candace said anxiously.

Jessica took the small neatly wrapped box from the bag and slowly untied it.

"Girl it looks like Mr. Keith has no intentions of letting you go. The sparkle from that box is blinding my eyes. Well take them out and try them on," Candace said, leaning over to get a closer look at the earrings. "Jessica, they are gorgeous. I can tell they are not cheap."

"No they're not. These beauties cost fifteen hundred dollars. I saw them in Reese's Jewelers in New York during one of our trips there. He promised me he would buy them for me, but I wanted it to be a happy occasion. Besides the fact that I still care about him, it's the thoughtful things that he does like this that make it so difficult to get over him."

"Hey, are you going to try them on or not?" Candace said reaching for the box.

"No Candace, I'm not going to try on the earrings. This is all a bit much for me to swallow," she said, closing the box. "We'd better get back to work before we get in trouble for being tardy."

"Hey Miss Jessica!" Clyde shouted, waving her to the desk. "The florist loves you today."

"Thanks Clyde. She signed for the flowers and walked away quickly. A smile came over her face when she read the card that came with her one yellow rose.

Happy Birthday Jessica. I'll call you later. I'd like to take you out to celebrate your birthday. Jehu.

At home Jessica admired the rose that Jehu sent her. She sat on the side of the bed and looked at the small box that Keith had given her. The phone rang and it was Keith. Her heart said yes, but her mind said no. She took a deep breath and answered.

"Keith, you must stop this. It's over and I mean it."

"Jessica, listen, please listen."

"No Keith", you listen. I cannot come back to you. There is no future for us. I don't want to see or hear from you again. Is that clear?"

"But Jessica—"

No Keith, she interrupted. "This is final. You have truly hurt me, but I'm going on with my life. Letting you back in would be a great mistake. Good bye Keith," she said gently hanging up the phone. Just as she was reaching for the mail on the table, the phone rang again. This time it was someone that she wanted to talk to.

"Hello."

"Happy birthday Jessica."

"Thank you Jehu. I'm enjoying the beautiful rose and card."

"I would like to take you out for an enjoyable evening to celebrate your birthday. I hope you will allow me to pick the place, because I would like for it to be a surprise. Is that alright with you?"

"Yes, that sounds wonderful. I like surprises."

"How about Saturday around seven? That will give us more time and we won't have to rush the evening."

"Sounds good. I'll see you then." Jessica hung up the phone. She couldn't wait until Saturday.

CHAPTER SEVENTEEN

Jessica's heart pounded as she eyed Jehu through her peripheral vision as they drove along. She tried to look calm but she felt like a little girl waiting to open her Christmas present.

"Brother Jehu, are you sure you can't let me in on your secret?"

"I thought we agreed that you would drop the brother act. Just Jehu is fine, okay?"

And fine you are, she thought.

"Of course, Jehu. I like that better as well."

"This is not a secret, but a surprise. Trust me; I think you will be pleased."

"Why won't you tell me where we're going? I'm not sure if I'm properly dressed."

"Don't worry, you look good enough to go anywhere, and I mean anywhere," he said glancing over at her with a smile. "If you don't feel comfortable once we're at our destination, we can leave. Is that fair enough?"

"Fair enough," she said, relaxing in her seat.

He turned his silver Lexus into a secured complex and entered the garage. "No questions," he said raising his hand to Jessica as she opened her mouth to speak. "Just follow me. Okay?"

"Alright," she said letting him take the lead.

He opened the door for her admiring her long shapely legs as she turned her body to exit the car. They entered the elevator from the parking garage and went to the eighth floor. He opened the door and gestured for her to go in.

"Wow, this is beautiful Jehu. Everything is so meticulously placed." Jessica was amazed. The bamboo floor in both the living and dining rooms looked great with the midnight blue six piece leather sofa; nicely accented with dark wood tables, a few colorful pictures on the wall, and a beautiful oak book case that covered one wall of the room. Just from a quick scan she could see that he had a great selection of books on history, religion, cooking and some novels. The dining room table setting looked like something you would see in a magazine.

"Jehu, the table setting is lovely. This is quite a surprise," she said, releasing her shawl to him.

"Thank you my lady," he said taking her arm and tucking it inside his arm as he escorted her into the kitchen.

Oh my! That fragrance and his abs showing through his shirt are making it difficult to focus. I plan to find out who Jehu Edwards really is tonight. This red dress with the three inch matching heels really should work for me tonight.

"I love your kitchen. Did you hire a decorator?"

"I had a little help from Mom, but I did most of it myself," he said guiding her to be seated at the counter.

"I spent a lot of time in the kitchen growing up. My mom and dad divorced when I was five. My sister is four years older than me and when she left for college, I bonded even more with Mom. When my friends came over, I did the cooking, made the snacks and cleaned the kitchen, of course."

"The girls must have been very impressed with your skills in the kitchen," she said, reaching for the glass of wine he sat in front of her.

"I was very shy in school, so the girls weren't really into me, especially since I didn't chase after them. Most of them thought I was gay."

The happy expression on her face faded instantly. "What happened to make them think that?"

"Well, when I didn't ask Janice Hall, the most popular cheerleader at Neely High, to go to the football dance, she started the rumor that I was gay."

"How did you handle that?"

"At first I was devastated. I even lost a few friends. But my wonderful mother helped me by praying with me and reminding me that as long as I knew who I was and God knew, the opinion of others didn't matter."

"It sounds like your mother gave you some wonderful values to live by."

"Yes, she did and I love her for it. Now let's decide on dinner," he said putting on his chef's apron and sliding a small menu in front of her. "You have a choice. Take a look and decide."

"This is better than a restaurant. I get a personal waiter and cook all wrapped in one."

Maybe even the man too, she thought. "Everything looks good. Let me see, grilled chicken salad or salmon with grilled vegetables, mashed potatoes and a garden salad. How about a grilled salmon salad with blue cheese dressing?"

"You may have whatever you like. This is your special night," he said placing his hand on her shoulder.

Careful guy, a statement like that means I can put you on the menu also. Dessert perhaps?

The dining room table setting was perfect with lighted candles and a small wrapped gift placed next to Jessica's plate.

"You may open that after dinner."

"You're in charge Brother Jehu," she said laughing. "Everything is just the way I like it. Your menu idea is original, but what if I didn't want anything on your menu?"

"I anticipated that and I have some gourmet entrees in the freezer and there's a great French restaurant down the street that delivers."

"Everything is delicious Jehu."

"Would you like dessert?"

"I would love dessert, but I need to wait a while to give the main course a chance to digest. How about a tour of your condo while we wait?"

"You've seen everything except the upstairs where the bedroom and master bath are."

"You have such a lovely place. I'd like to see it all, but if you rather not, I understand."

"Come with me. I did say you could have whatever you want. This is your night."

She followed him up the winding staircase to the space that revealed his king sized bed and accessories.

My goodness, he looks good going and coming. Refocus Jessica, she thought.

Jessica immediately turned her focus to the French doors that led to the balcony with a beautiful landscaped view. A charcoal grey down-filled comforter with black and silver pillows covered his king size platform bed with built in LED lights around the platform. White plush wall-to-wall carpet covered the floor.

"You have really great taste Jehu. Did your mother help you with the decorating?"

"No, I thought it best to keep Mom out of my bedroom décor for fear it might start looking like hers," he smiled. "She's still a little old fashioned in some ways."

"You have such great taste Jehu. I love it" She pointed toward the bathroom for permission to enter. "Oh my, this tub is big enough for two people."

"It's a Jacuzzi and I wanted it to be big enough for two," he smiled shyly. Their eyes met and just for a moment she thought he would kiss her, but he turned and walked away.

"Well that's the end of the tour," he said, guiding her toward the stairs. "Would you like to look through the music selection while I get dessert?"

"Another surprise," she said heading down the staircase.

"How does peach cobbler sound?"

"Homemade and warm with ice cream?" she asked excitedly.

"Is there any other way to eat peach cobbler?" he said, giving her a wink.

He had a classy way of doing things that just set him apart from the kind of guys Jessica had known in the past. She was lucky if she got dinner from most of them, especially at a classy restaurant. Peach cobbler is not something the average man would even consider serving for dessert. She was beginning to feel that Jehu was not your average guy.

"I'm really enjoying this cobbler. Did you make it?"

"I most certainly did. I used my Mom's recipe. I'm glad you like it." He slid the small wrapped box in front of her. It was from Courtney's, one of the finest jewelers in town.

"Do I have your permission to open this now?"

"Yes, you may now open it."

Inside was a gold charm bracelet with one charm. He reached over to fasten it around her wrist. "I want this bracelet to represent memorable events in your life. The cross represents your salvation; your acceptance of Jesus Christ as your Lord and Savior."

"Thank you. It is beautiful," she said holding her wrist up to admire it.

"I hope that our relationship will grow to the point where I can be a part of helping you to choose the other charms."

"I hope so too," she responded.

This is where you kiss me guy, just like they do in the movies.

'He gently kissed her hand. "You're special Jessica. That's why I wanted everything to be special tonight. I hope you are really enjoying the evening."

"This was the best birthday celebration I have ever had."

"I'm glad. Unfortunately we have to bring it to an end because we have church tomorrow and I don't want to be the reason that you're late. I'll drive you home."

Home, who wants to go home? Isn't this when the real party starts? What about the kiss that I've been longing for? I'm really falling for you guy, so you better not be on the down low.

Lord, please say it isn't so!

"You're awfully quiet Jessica. I hope I didn't feed you too much," he said as he pulled in front of her condo. "This has been a fun and exciting evening. I'd like to see you again."

"I would like that also Jehu," she said blushing. She could feel her heart pounding.

This has got to be the moment, she thought. *We can finally get past the hand holding and the flirting eye contact. Come on Jehu; let the real man step up to bat!*

"Great! I look forward to it. Good night and sleep well." He leaned forward and kissed her on the cheek and held the door open for her to go inside. So far he had proven to her that he was not like the other guys she had gone out with, but he hadn't convinced her that the rumors about him were false.

CHAPTER EIGHTEEN

"My subject today is *Obedience is What God Wants From Us Most*," Reverend Anderson said.

Jessica listened attentively as he explained the importance of adhering to God's word and the consequences of disobedience. When he described what heaven was like, it really sounded like a place she would like to go, but the more she learned about God and what he expected of her, the more she was convinced that she couldn't live up to his standards. Loving your neighbor as you love yourself definitely meant her neighbors were out of luck, because she wasn't sure she loved herself.

"God made you, he loves you and he expects you to obey him," Reverend Anderson shouted. He turned his head in Jessica's direction as if he was addressing her. "He is a forgiving God. If you mess up, and you will; he will forgive you if you ask him. He will forget all about what you did. He doesn't hold grudges like some of us do. You'll have to sacrifice some things that you really want or want to do, but you will be greatly rewarded on earth and in heaven."

God really requires a lot from you, Jessica thought. *How do I know he'll hold up his end of the bargain? Is God really who they say he is or is he some fictitious character that I'm being brain washed to believe in. How do I know if he can really prove himself?*

She looked across the aisle at Jehu who was peering out the corner of his eye at her.

He looks good, talks good, smells good, and cooks good, but how do I know he's worth the wait?

After Bible class, she found Candace engrossed in a conversation with Albert in the corridor, so she walked quickly past her and headed for the ladies room.

"Candace, it's been weeks and I miss you. Why are you ignoring me and making me feel like a fool in front of everyone?" Albert said.

"I'm sorry Albert. It's not my intention. I just have a lot on my mind right now and—"

"And I have you on my mind. I want to spend some time with you. You're spending more time with your girlfriend than with me."

"I'm just trying to make her feel comfortable. She's a new saint and you know how some of the sisters hate on you if you look nice."

"Yes I know, but when can we get together? Let's go out and have some fun and…

"Yea, yea, okay Albert. I'll call you tonight and we can choose a time that will be good for both of us. Okay?"

"Alright," Albert said hesitantly. "I'll talk to you later."

Jessica was about to make her exit from the ladies room when she heard the door open. She heard two women talking, so she waited and listened.

"Sherry, why do you need to remake your face? We're not stopping anywhere special," Debbie remarked. "It's really not going to make a difference anyway."

"Talk about me if you want. I know you wore that low cut dress because you're hoping Brother Jehu might look your way," Sherry fired back.

"Yes Jehu, that is a fine brother," Debbie said, checking her full figure in the mirror.

"Unfortunately he doesn't seem to be interested in you or any other female," Sherry snickered.

Neither of them bothered to check to see if anyone was in the toilet area. Jessica was glad that she was able to over hear what they were saying.

"Oh Sherry you need to stop spreading gossip. Even if he is on the down low, prayer can fix that and you know I am willing to intercede for him." Debbie adjusted the front of her dress that revealed the most noticeable part of her body.

"I heard he's been spending quality time with the new chick. What's her name? Joyce? Jan? No it's Jessica," Sherry recalled. "I've seen several of the brothers admiring her. They're all like dogs, always looking for a fresh bone when they haven't tried the one right in their reach."

Debbie paused from admiring herself in the mirror. "Isn't she also taking the teaching classes?"

"Yes and Mean Millie is mentoring her," Sherry said. They both laughed and Sherry paused before touching up her lipstick.

"Millie told Betty that she doesn't have what it takes to be a good teacher. She's only working with her because First Lady Anderson asked her to. There's a bitter pill hiding behind those sugary hellos that Sister Millie sends out. I heard the situation that landed her husband in the wheelchair almost took her over the edge."

Debbie took a final look at herself and moved toward the door. "Well when Millie is done with her, I'm sure she'll be looking for another church and I'll have Brother Jehu all to myself since everyone else is afraid. I think the brother is just being cautious. Come on Sherry before you over do your face."

The door closed and Jessica waited a few minutes before exiting.

CHAPTER NINETEEN

"Good afternoon Ladies."

"Hello Reverend Ben," Jessica and Candace said in unison.

"You ladies look so nice. Were you blessed by the message today?"

"Yes I was," remarked Jessica.

"Yes, it was a great sermon Reverend Ben," Candace chimed in loudly. "Your sermons always inspire me."

"Thank you. That is wonderful to hear. Enjoy the rest of your day ladies." He turned to walk in the opposite direction, and then suddenly stopped. "Sister Jessica, will you be attending Wednesday night Bible study?"

"Yes it's on my schedule."

"I was wondering if you could arrive about fifteen minutes early and stop by my office. I'd like to speak with you on a matter."

"Yes, of course Reverend Ben," Jessica answered giving Candace a quick puzzled look.

"I'll see you then." They watched him walk away.

"So you're after my man," Candace said. I can't believe you would do that right in front of me."

"Give it a rest Candace. He just asked me to stop by his office to talk. I don't have any interest in Reverend Ben."

"Maybe you don't, but he's sure interested in you. Don't tell me you haven't noticed it."

Jessica didn't want to admit that she had noticed how Reverend Ben looked at her, so she tried to change the subject. "Oh girl, he probably just wants to give me some project to work on. You know I offered to help out wherever I'm needed."

"Yea, sure Miss Jessica."

Jessica planned to keep her word to meet with Reverend Ben, but just in case he wanted to get personal, she had to prepare herself. They headed toward the door and it was no doubt that Candace was angry. She was never without words and Jessica could hear her breathing heavy as she walked quickly ahead of her.

"Are we still on for lunch tomorrow Candace?"

"Yea, sure Miss man stealer. We can discuss your strategy for taking your best friends man."

Jessica couldn't believe Candace was accusing her of someone that she was not dating, nor had he made any commitment to do so. She was fed up with being falsely accused.

"He's not your man and I'm not after him. It's not my fault that he's not showing the interest in you that you want him to." Jessica's voice escalated to a loud volume not conducive to indoors. "You think you can get any man you want, but every man that you want doesn't necessarily want you."

Candace walked ahead of Jessica, holding her right hand up signifying that she was no longer listening to her. Tears filled Jessica's eyes. She tried to hold them back but they slowly rolled down her face.

"I hate to see a pretty lady cry," the man standing behind her said.

Now she had a man observing her at a vulnerable moment. She turned cautiously to see who was speaking. She tried to wipe the tears from her eyes with her hand as she fumbled in her purse for a tissue. When she was able to focus, she turned to see King standing there with a sympathetic look.

"King I'm sorry, this is not a good time to chat. I really have to go."

"Please, allow me," he said handing her a nice pressed white handkerchief.

"Are you okay?"

"Yes, I'm fine. Thanks for your concern." She didn't feel comfortable talking to King about her problem with Candace. Right now she didn't want to talk to anyone. She couldn't understand where the tears came from. She and Candace had words in the pass, but they managed to forgive and go on with their friendship. They had never had an argument over a man. "Excuse me, I must be going," she said abruptly.

"May I see you to your car?"

"It's just a few feet away, she said pointing to the silver grey convertible Toyota Solara.

"Whatever the problem, God has an answer for you in his word. Try reading Matthew, chapter 6, verse 33 and chapter 7, verses 7 and 8.

"Thank you for the advice. I'll do that." She walked silently to her car. King stood watching her until she drove away.

CHAPTER TWENTY

Candace swished past Jessica looking straight ahead. A few co-workers looked on in surprise as Jessica turned her attention to the ringing phone on her desk.

"Henry North Hospital, how may I help you?" Jessica answered.

As much as she tried to focus on work, Keith's persistence and Candace's rejection was occupying her mind more than she wanted to admit. She looked around for Candace in the cafeteria at lunch time. She never missed fish and mac and cheese day. Just as she was placing her empty tray on the tray line, she spotted Candace.

"Candace, please talk to me. How can you allow some man to come between years of friendship? You know I'm not interested in Reverend Ben. Candace, please," she begged.

Candace waved her off and continued walking. Jessica didn't want to eat lunch alone and by now it seemed everyone was staring at her. She decided to skip lunch and go for a short walk. She really needed someone to talk to, but Candace had always been her sounding board. The busy afternoon made the day go by faster, but she was not looking forward to another lonely night alone and not having your best friend to talk to.

Jessica sat in her big chair by the window pondering over how she lost her best friend. The phone rang and she hoped it was Candace, but it was Jehu.

"Jehu, I'm glad you called."

"Well convince me that you're glad to hear from me because you sound more like you're sorry I called."

"Forgive me, I'm not in the best mood and I could certainly use a friend, especially since I seem to have lost my best friend."

"I'm all ears. What's the matter?"

"Candace stopped speaking to me."

"Why?"

"She accused me of trying to take her man."

"I wasn't aware that she was seeing anyone special. So who is he?"

"She's got this notion that Reverend Ben likes her even though he hasn't said so or even asked her out. Sunday after church, he asked me to stop by his office after Wednesday night Bible class so he could talk to me about something. On another Sunday he was greeting me and she said he was holding my hand too long. Honest Jehu, I haven't given Reverend Ben a thought. I have noticed that he has a tendency to flirt, but that happens with other women in the church."

"Yes, I have noticed that as well and although he is single, as a minister he should be careful about the signals he sends out to the women."

"I can't convince her that she's wrong. I tried talking to her at work today and she just waved me off and kept walking."

"Jessica, I'm so sorry to hear that you and Candace are having a disagreement. This is something you really need to pray about. Affairs of the heart have long been the catalyst for dissolving relationships. Ask God to touch Candace's heart and reveal the truth to her. I believe that Candace is rooted enough in the word to hear God and it's time for you to believe that God answers prayers."

"I'm not sure I know how to pray or that God would hear me if I did."

"Jessica, God always hears your prayers. He may not answer them the way you want him to or even when you want him to. Your heavenly father loves you and only wants the best for you."

"Will you," she said hesitating, "pray with me?"

"Of course I will. Let's do that right now."

It sounded as if he was talking to a real person that he knew him well. He kept reminding him of what he had said in his word about forgiveness and trust and other things that she had heard Reverend Anderson preach about. She felt so much better after he prayed for her.

This guy not only looks good, smells good, and cooks well, but prays to God like he has a personal relationship with Him. What a guy!

CHAPTER TWENTY-ONE

"Candace, I didn't know you could cook. Dinner was delicious; almost as good as you," Albert said reaching over to kiss her.

"Albert," she said, pulling away from him. "We need to talk. That's why I asked you to have dinner here. I didn't want any interruptions."

"What's wrong sweetness? Did I do something wrong? You know I would never intentionally do something to make you angry or hurt you. You know that Candace."

"Yes Albert I know that. It's not what you have done, but what we have been doing. We both know that we are sinning before God with our little sexual encounters. The guilt is making me nauseous. We have to stop Albert."

"Candace, I know you're right, but what are you saying. Does this mean that you are breaking up with me? I love you Candace and I thought you loved me too. I—I don't know what to say. You refused my marriage proposal and now you want to just kick me to the curve altogether. Candace, please don't do this. Tell me that's not what you're saying."

She reached over and held both of Albert's hands and looked into his eyes. "Albert I want to apologize for the way I have been treating you. You did nothing to deserve it. I do love you and I have been very selfish about our relationship. I want to give some more thought to our getting married. Let us both pray about this. I know I'm the one that has been putting things on hold, but I need to make sure that I do the right thing for both our sakes. It's imperative that I believe that I can be a good wife to you Albert. Do you understand what I'm saying?"

"I think so Candace," he answered. "I believe that you would be just what I need. I know that I'm not everything that you probably want in a man, but Candace I will treat you like a queen. I'm not tall, dark and handsome," he laughed. "I've heard some of the ladies make that statement. But baby I don't believe anyone can love you more than me and I'll work two jobs if that is what it takes to get you all the things you desire." He reached in his pocket and pulled out the ring that Candace had refused to take from him last year. "What do I have to do for you take this ring? You see, I haven't given up."

Candace held out her left hand for Albert to place the ring on her finger. He was so nervous and excited that she had to help him.

"Albert we have to go through counseling with Reverend Anderson. We need to really get to know each other better and talk about things that we have never really touched on, like family, friends, finances, likes and dislikes. Now we need to start having real dates, without the sex, until we're married. Can you handle that?"

"Baby, I can handle it all. Whatever you say. Can I at least get a kiss?" he said reluctantly.

"Sure honey, but not one of those long ones that will get us off focus." Albert gave her a gentle kiss on the lips and held her close to him. "I love you Candace and I want you to be my wife."

Candace couldn't believe what she had just done, but she knew it was the right thing to do and God was pleased. She was definitely not going to make an announcement to the church, although she knew the minute one person saw the ring and learned that Albert was her fiancé, it would be big news. She had to get her attitude right for all of the negative comments that she knew was coming. This was a time that she really needed her friend Jessica to talk to and it was her fault that they were not speaking.

CHAPTER TWENTY-TWO

"Jessica, please come in. How are you doing? Please be seated," Reverend Ben said.

"Fine, Reverend Ben," Jessica replied as she sat down.

"I'll get right to the point Jessica. We're forming a committee for the pastor's anniversary next year and I thought adding a new member would be good; someone to help give us old timers some fresh ideas. We don't have anyone in your age group on the committee and frankly the members come every year with the program from the previous year as a model. I'd like to see something different," he said pausing for Jessica's response.

"Well," Jessica said clearing her throat. "I'm grateful that you are considering me, but I don't think that I would be able to bring anything fresh or otherwise to the table. I've never done anything like this before. Most of the people know each other and have something in common. I only know a handful of people and frankly Reverend Ben, I don't feel comfortable getting involved in something like that right now. I'd like to focus on Bible classes and the training I'm getting from Sister Millie. I plan to teach someday." She noticed Reverend Ben's eyes were shifting from her face to her legs. She tried to discreetly pull her skirt closer to her knees.

"Perhaps getting involved will help you get to know more people and in turn they can get to know you."

"I'm sorry Reverend Ben. I'm just not ready for that yet," she said standing up.

"Please pray about it Jessica and let me know if you change your mind," he said reaching for her hand and placing the other hand on top. "I know you'll make a great teacher. Let me know if I can help in any way."

"Thank you, I will," Jessica said loosening the grip of his hand as she headed out the door.

"Hello pretty lady."

Jessica looked up to see King standing by the kiosk. "Oh hello Mr. Jordan."

"King," he reminded her.

"Yes, King. How are you?"

"I'm fine. I'm surprised to see you here so late and without your sidekick. I saw her leave right after Bible class."

"There are times when we're not together. We do have separate lives," Jessica said sarcastically.

"Are you two having a disagreement?"

"You might say that, but it's not something that we can't work out."

"You shouldn't let a man interfere with your friendship."

"You shouldn't think that the only conversations we have are about men."

"Wow! You are a feisty pretty lady. I apologize. I didn't mean any harm. I've known Candace for a while now and—well just pardon my assumption."

"What is it with you and Candace? You say you have known her for a while and she acts as if you are her enemy," Jessica said, pausing for King's response.

"Candace picks her acquaintances very carefully. I'm not sure what the qualifications are but obviously I don't qualify," King said jokingly.

"Are you sure there wasn't a past fling and the two of you are hiding it?"

"I'm sure and it's not that I didn't try."

"It seems to me that two Christians should be able to get past their differences and at least be on speaking terms."

"I agree pretty lady, but your girlfriend doesn't see it that way. Perhaps that's something that you can pray about."

"There must be a lot of praying around here. I keep getting that suggestion every time I have a challenge."

"That's what Christians do. We pray a lot and some of us like to have fun, although some people believe that we live a boring life and only go to church."

"It's strange that you should say that, because that's exactly what I've always thought."

"I'd like to prove you wrong. Let me take you out for an evening of fun."

"I don't know King. This is quite unexpected. You really caught me off guard. I need to think about this." She never saw this coming. She actually believed King was interested in helping her grow in the word. In spite of what he says, she should never forget how men think.

"It'll just be an evening of fun. When is the last time you just went out for fun with a friend? Will you at least think about it?"

"I'll give it some thought. You have a good evening."

As she walked away, she could feel him watching her. This is just what she was accustomed to from men outside the church. She had hoped this church experience would be different.

CHAPTER TWENTY-THREE

Jessica checked herself in the mirror for the third time to make sure she was appropriately dressed for church. "Jessica," she said aloud, "Today you finally get to be a teacher, so don't mess up. I wish I could share my joy with Candace." She headed out to another uncertain moment in her life, but an opportunity that she was excited about.

"Jessica," Millie said beckoning her to the side. "The content of today's lesson is quite challenging. I thought it over and I think it would be best if I taught the class today. You've been doing great in your training but this session is not the best for a first timer. I don't want you to get in over your head."

"Well—well isn't that why you're here to help me if I need it? I know everyone knows that it's my first time and I have really studied and prepared for the class. Even you said at our last session that you thought I would do well," Jessica said with a frown.

"I know Jessica, but as I said we'll choose another class with a subject that's a little less challenging. Now we better get started. The class is waiting," Millie said patting her wig to make sure it was in place.

Jessica slowly walked over and sat in the back of the class. Members of the class turned to look back at her sympathetically.

"Sister Millie, I thought Jessica was teaching today," said Naomi. "What happened?"

"Jessica will teach at a later date," Millie replied. "Now let's get started."

"Um huh," Naomi replied rolling her eyes and nudging her talking buddy Anita with her elbow.

Jessica made her way to the ladies room as her eyes filled with tears.

"Jessica, honey what's wrong?" It was a voice that Jessica didn't recognize.

"Nothing, I'm fine," Jessica replied to the blurred face staring at her.

"Why don't you come to my office and sit until you feel better?"

"Evangelist Anna, I didn't recognize you. Thank you, but I'm fine," Jessica said wiping the tears from her eyes.

"No you're not and I insist you come with me," she said gently taking Jessica by the arm.

"Would you like some water Jessica?"

"Yes, thank you Evangelist Anna."

"I know we haven't had much conversation, but right now it seems you need someone to talk to. I'm a good listener and will keep our conversation confidential. I've watched you come diligently to Bible class and your teaching classes. Weren't you scheduled to teach today?"

"Yes, I was. Sister Millie decided this morning that it would be best for her to teach the class and that I wait for a class that was less challenging. I've worked so hard through much adversity, even from Sister Millie. God's word is so holy; maybe I'm not worthy to teach his word."

"Perhaps you have misinterpreted her actions," Evangelist Anna said. "I know what it's like to be the new Christian trying to fit in and expect the people in the church to want to help you and love you. But unfortunately all of the people won't live up to your expectations. They are all at a different place on their Christian journey."

"But do you really understand what I'm going through? I have been shunned by people who claim to love God and mistreated by some who claim to want to help me. Evangelist Anna, something is wrong with this picture."

"Jessica only God knows the true heart of his people. Only He knows who is saved and who is not. So the saved and the unsaved, the baby and the mature Christians, the good, bad and the ugly are all here together. But only the righteous shall see heaven. I pray that you will continue to dig deep into the word of God. It will help you get through this. Don't allow the adversity to make you bitter and angry. Learn to trust God to change you and show you how to deal with the enemy working through other people."

"Evangelist Anna, I appreciate you ministering to me although I'm not sure I understand it all. I don't know if I can handle this. I'm torn between doing what God says to do and what I want to do. It's so difficult to turn the other cheek when people mistreat you," she said reaching for another tissue.

"Jessica, I will help you. I'll pray with you. Feel free to call me if you need to talk. Don't forget that Pastor and First Lady Anderson have an open door policy and you can talk to them as well."

"You really don't know how I feel." Jessica sniffled and wiped her nose again.

"Yes I do Jessica. I was once you, feeling pretty much the same way you're feeling. Believe me when I came here with my black husband and child, I was not always well received because I was the only Hispanic in the church at that time. Then my husband left me after we had been here for three years. Thank God that I had been studying God's word and applying it to my life. Reverend Anderson and First Lady Anderson wrapped their arms around me and helped me get through the hurt and humiliation. Don't let people tell you who you are. Let the word of God do that."

"All this is so overwhelming. I need time to think, I—need to go. Thank you again Evangelist Anna."

Jessica hurried down the hall and out to her car. She was not in the mood for questions and people pretending to be sympathetic.

CHAPTER TWENTY-FOUR

Jessica tossed the idea of going out with King around in her mind. Although Jehu was showing a great interest in her, there was still that bit of uncertainty about him. He seemed too good to be true. She decided to keep her options open; after all, King did say it would just be friends going out for an evening of fun.

"Jessica you look ravishing," King said as he opened the car door to his black corvette and she slid her long legs inside. "I know you'll enjoy the musical and since it's a matinee I hope you don't mind that I made dinner reservations for seven."

"Sounds good. Where exactly will we be dining?"

"You said you are a seafood lover, so I thought you would like Danny's. It's one of the best places in town." Her silence was an indication that she had some challenges with his plans. "Is that okay with you?"

It was a place that Keith like to frequent. The possibility of running into Him or Jehu was not something she wanted to happen. She shuttered to think what the outcome of that might be. She really didn't want to take that chance.

"Actually my choice would be The Net. It's a little further out, but I'm familiar with their food. Do you mind?"

"Pretty lady, your wish is my command," he said pressing the speed dial on his cell phone. "I have a contact there so it shouldn't be a problem to get a last minute reservation."

Jessica was excited about seeing the stage version of Dream Girls. She had seen the movie and really enjoyed it. According to King, the community theater's cast was very good, so she expected that she would enjoy this as well. She could see King staring at her through her peripheral vision as she settled into her seat at the theater.

"Are you comfortable?" he asked touching her leg and quickly removing his hand.

"Yes, thank you," she replied repositioning herself in her seat.

The seating was actually nice for a community theater. She compared each character in the play to the actors from the movie. Each stage character had some of the same characteristics as those in the movie, except for the lady who played Effie White. She was tall and slender, unlike the original character that was very robust in size. This actress also had a nice strong voice that also earned her a standing ovation when she sang the song, *I'm Not Living Without You.*

The play was over and Jessica was ready for dinner. She loved the ambiance of The Net, especially the carpeted floor and cherry wood around the edges of the wall. The piped in music playing softly was an added incentive. She discreetly scanned the room for familiar faces. She couldn't understand why she felt as if she was cheating? Neither Keith nor Jehu should be in her thoughts when she had this man right in front of her giving her all of his attention.

"King you were right. I really enjoyed the musical. It was excellent," she smiled nodding to the waiter to fill her cup with coffee.

"Does that mean that we can do this again soon?"

"It certainly is a possibility."

"The flowers are beautiful', she said, looking around the room to find that only their table had them.

"I'm glad you like them. Beautiful flowers for a beautiful lady. I had them put here just for you."

"Wow, I feel so special," she smiled.

'That's because you are very special," he said looking directly into her eyes and touching her hand on the table.

She scanned the room for the two men that she had unleashed her heart to; one leaving her hurt and the other with mixed feelings. She was totally unaware that the waiter was standing patiently waiting to take her order.

"Jessica, are you ready to order?" King said.

"Oh, yes of course. I'll have the lobster tail removed from the shell, chopped salad, almond green beans and the twice baked potato with sour cream and butter."

"Sam, I would like the sirloin, medium well, garlic mashed potatoes, grilled mushrooms and the house salad with vinaigrette. Please make sure the bread is warm."

"Yes Mr. Jordan," the waiter said retrieving their menus.

"Mr. King, I never would have guessed that you were a meat and potatoes man," Jessica smiled.

"Mr. King," he said laughing and raising one eyebrow. "I thought we had passed the formality."

"We have indeed Mr. King. Just a little humor."

"You're quite a kidder, aren't you?"

"Only with people I feel comfortable with. Now back to our conversation about your order. I thought we were both having seafood."

"Unfortunately I'm allergic."

"Sorry to hear that. You're really missing some delicious meals."

"Yes I know, but I found out the hard way."

"You have whatever you want. This is your night, Jessica, and I want you to be pleased in every way."

There was a moment of silence as they drank their coffee and Jessica tried to pretend that King wasn't constantly looking at her.

"King," she said breaking the silence. "Why aren't you married or in a committed relationship?"

"You might say that my failed marriage left me hesitant to do it again. I haven't really met anyone that I thought could change my mind until now."

"Until now, what do you mean?"

"You must know that you have captured my heart."

"I'm flattered King, but I had no idea that you felt this way. I don't know what to say," she said nervously.

"I hope you will give our friendship a chance to blossom into something that we both can commit to."

"I'm really not ready to—I'm not sure I can give you the answer you want to hear. You know I've been seeing someone else."

"Oh yes, I know about Brother Jehu, but because you're here with me instead of him tells me the brother hasn't made a commitment yet or you're not sure about your feelings," he said with a look of confidence on his face.

"Waiter, please bring us a bottle of Dom Pérignon. It may be a bit premature, but we're having a celebration," he grinned.

"No King, you asked me to think about it, so let's not start celebrating."

"Let's just have a toast to the possibility. I would never force you into anything. I will honor whatever you decide. Alright?"

He looked at her with those dark brown eyes waiting for her to respond.

He had such a calming effect on her when he spoke with such gentleness in his deep voice.

"Alright, but don't try to get me drunk. Remember, I'm not the new girl in the neighborhood. I know most of the tricks," she said giving him a wink. The waiter arrived with the food and Jessica was relieved that she could change the conversation.

Jessica didn't want the fun part of the evening to end, but as they pulled in front of her condo, she was relieved that she wouldn't have to keep pretending that King's subtle advances weren't inviting to her. "Thank you for a wonderful evening King," she said as he opened the door leading to the lobby. "I'll be fine from here."

"A gentleman always makes sure a lady gets to her apartment safely," he said as he continued walking with her to the elevator. Jessica put the key in the door, stepped inside and turned around to say goodnight. His lips met hers and she didn't resist as he moved closer to her closing the door behind them. Jessica had no thoughts of Keith or Jehu, just Mr. King.

CHAPTER TWENTY-FIVE

The pillow next to her was damp with his perspiration. She lay still with her eyes closed inhaling his scent. That side of the bed had been empty since she stopped seeing Keith. She sat up and looked around; hoping that last night had not turned into a bad morning that she would regret. A note on the night stand caught her eye. She picked it up and read it aloud.

"Pretty Lady, it was a wonderful night. See you at church. King"

Now it was all clear. Too much champagne and a charismatic persuasive man equals a temporary good time.

"My God, what have I done?" Her heart felt as if it dropped to her stomach, much like the same nauseating feeling she experienced when she received the phone call from Keith's wife, but much worse. This time she had involved God in her mess and she was afraid of the consequences.

Her life had become a bigger mess than it was before she came to Mercy Seat. She had lost her best friend because of the flirtations of a preacher that never verbalized an interest in either of them. How could he do such misleading things and how could Candace get lured in by his meaningless gestures? Sister Millie had embarrassed her in front of the entire Sunday school class and now the whole church probably knew about her failed attempt to teach God's word. The man she was falling for couldn't make a commitment to her and his sexuality was questionable. Now she had yielded to temptation with King Jordan and it would probably be top gossip at Mercy Seat before long. She had allowed her physical needs to get in the way of God's plan for her life. What will Jehu think when he finds out, or should she care? After all, King was just willing to do what he wouldn't, but she was angry that King befriended her on the pretense of being interested in her spiritual growth. Now she knows he was just baiting her to get what all the other men that slid through her life wanted. She was beginning to like King, although he couldn't replace the spot in her heart for Jehu. There was no way she could open her mouth to ask God to forgive her and she certainly wasn't going to his house to pretend that she was holy and righteous. The membership in the righteous club was already overflowing. In the past when she had a crisis she could call Candace. Now Candace was part of the crisis and calling her was not an option. She held her pounding head in her hands as she sat in the big chair by the window to gather her thoughts. There were no medications in the house, not even an aspirin.

Nobody loves me. If I disappeared, no one would miss me. Maybe I should just end this right now and be done with it.

Her stove was electric, so she couldn't turn on the gas. She was too much of a chicken to hang herself or jump out of the window. It would be her luck that she would only break a leg or arm if she jumped and then all the neighbors would know. Cutting her wrist would only add to the pain.

"Keith kept a bottle of Grand Marnier Cordon Rouge in the cabinet," she spoke aloud. She remembered it was the only thing that she hadn't thrown out that reminded her of him, and that was because it was out of sight. Maybe if she got drunk enough, she would have the nerve to bring her miserable life to an end. After the first glass, she began to like the taste and the pain was subsiding. By the fourth glass the pain was gone, but her stomach started to rebel against the sweet, strong alcoholic beverage. Once again her attempt to rid herself of the pain in her life had failed.

CHAPTER TWENTY-SIX

Jessica couldn't face the people at Mercy Seat, especially King. Several weeks had passed and she kept to herself, except for work. Her voicemail was full of sales calls, messages from Jehu, King and one call from Sister Anna, encouraging her to come back to church. She didn't know what was worse, the isolation or the thought of actually going back to Mercy seat. All the thoughts flowing through her head were making her feel crazy. Her head felt like it was going to explode and she wanted someone else to feel the mental and physical pain that she was experiencing; preferably the person that was responsible. She had downsized to a size eight from a perfect size ten, which she had proudly maintained from her teen years. Her meals had been consisting of water, juice and an occasional bagel. She wasn't talking to anyone besides the people at work that she had to talk to in order to do her job. Now was the time that she really needed to find out if this God she had been learning about was really who they say he is. She had nothing to lose by trying to communicate with him, so she spoke aloud to him. "God, where are you now? If you are everywhere and know everything, don't you know I'm hurting and I need help? Do I have to ask you for help? You're Almighty God. There's nothing too hard for you. Can you just take the pain away? Please God! Please!"

She waited to see if she could hear God speaking back to her, but there was only silence and the sounds of the world outside just passing her by. The telephone rang and she checked the caller ID to see who was calling. It was King calling again. She hadn't seen or spoken to him since the week end that she met the real King Jordan. She knew she had to face him sooner or later.

"Hello," she answered,

"Jessica, I've been worried about you. Are you alright?"

"Yes." The one word answer was her way of letting him know that she really didn't want to talk to him.

"Why haven't you answered my calls? You haven't been to church and—"

"Isn't it obvious," she interrupted. "I don't want to be bothered with you because that's what got me in the trouble I'm in now. I don't want any more contact with you or Mercy Seat."

"I care about you Jessica and I believe you have feelings for me as well. Can we at least talk about this?"

"No, we can't."

"I want to be a part of your life. You need a good man to stand by you and encourage you because God has great plans for your future in teaching his word. You'll bring teaching to a new level at Mercy Seat."

"Still prophesying King? Why didn't you prophesy about our little escapade rather than lure me into a situation that you knew was wrong? If you really care about me, why did you take advantage of me? You knew I was vulnerable and struggling to stay free from my previous lifestyle. You used my weakness to get what you wanted. Now I'm hurting and afraid to ask God for forgiveness because I don't believe he will." Her voice faded as the tears rolled down her face.

"Jessica, I'm sorry. I should have walked away when you asked me to, but I allowed my feelings to control my actions that night. Can you forgive me?"

"I don't know," she said, disconnecting the call.

CHAPTER TWENTY-SEVEN

Jessica sat in the big chair by the window. Her mind roamed from Jehu, to Candace, to King and then to Keith. All of these people played a part in the pain she was feeling. There had to be a way out of this mind boggling, heart wrenching situation. She wanted to scream, but had no energy and no voice. She ignored the doorbell that kept interrupting her clouded thoughts. She wasn't expecting company and didn't want to talk to anyone, especially King Jordan. The persistency of the bell ringing was annoying.

"Whoever you are, go away," she yelled into the intercom.

"Jessica, I'm going to be here until you talk to me if it takes all night."

She recognized Jehu's voice. The man she really cared about was as close as opening the door. If she let him in what would she say? Telling him about King would be the worst thing she could do right now. What if he is the right man for her? She could ruin her chances of them ever getting together.

"Jessica, I'm waiting," he said with authority. She had never heard him speak in that tone before.

"Jessica whatever the problem is, it can be worked out. Don't let the devil shut you out from God, you need him. And don't let him shut you out from me. I need you too."

"I don't need anyone and God hates me," she yelled. "He won't answer my prayers and right now I'm not talking to him either."

"Jessica I need you. You know I care about you. Please let me in so we can talk. I'm here for you. Closing yourself off from people only allows the devil to taunt you more. You can't fight the enemy with anger and bitterness. Now buzz me in. I'm going to stay here all night if I have to."

She knew he was right because she had no idea how to fight the evil one and some of the things going through her mind were certainly not Godly thoughts. She recalled Reverend Anderson's teaching about God keeping you in perfect peace. Peace was definitely not in her house and she knew why.

Several people had entered the building while Jehu was trying to convince Jessica to let him in. A strikingly beautiful young lady who reminded him of Jessica in stature with the long flowing hair stopped to speak to him. She had obviously heard his conversation with Jessica.

"A fine brother like you shouldn't be begging. You can come in with me and I'll treat you right," she said smiling.

There was a time in his life when he would have yielded to the temptation, but that season of his life had ended. He just smiled.

"Apartment 605, code 201 in case you change your mind," she said walking away swaying her hips and giving him a wink.

"Jehu, are you still there?"

"Yes Jessica, I'm still here and will be here until you let me in."

"Come on up, but don't try to convince me to go back to Mercy Seat." She pondered over whether she would say what is really in her heart or just wait to see what he has to say. The tap on the door left her no time to rehearse.

"Come in. Would you like something to drink, water, soda or tea," she said avoiding direct eye contact.

"Cold water would be nice. It's thirsty work trying to break into this building." They both laughed as he pulled her into his arms and held her.

"Jessica, promise me you won't ever shut yourself off like that again."

Right now I'll promise you anything if you keep holding me like this, she thought.

"Nothing can be so bad that you can't get through it with God's help. I've been so concerned about you, and when you wouldn't answer my calls, I almost got angry with you. I had no one that I could ask about you, so here I am."

Yes and this is just where I want you. I had to get crazy to get you to put your arms around me. My, my, my, this is better than I imagined.

Her mind raced along with the heavy pounding of her heart. "I promise because I don't want anyone calling the police on you. I really missed you Jehu, but try to understand that I just don't want to discuss my problems with anyone. I tried talking to God, but I don't think he's listening. Is he listening Jehu? Will he hear me? Why doesn't he answer me? I thought he loved me?"

"Of course he's listening. God loves you Jessica and wants nothing but the best for you. He knows you're hurting and he knows why. I promise you, if you go to God believing that he will help you; he will. We don't understand why God does things the way he does. His timing is never as we would want or predict, but it's always right. This is why we have to trust Him and not in things or ourselves."

"What about you Jehu? Will you help me?"

"Yes, of course. I will help you in any way I can."

She held him tighter as if that would assure her that she would never lose him.

"But right now I could use a cold drink," he said, loosening her grip on him. "Water is fine."

She slowly moved away from him and retrieved a bottle of cold water from her empty refrigerator. They had been talking for hours when they realized it was late and they hadn't eaten.

"Do you have anything here that resembles food," he said rubbing his stomach.

"Sorry, eating has been one of the things that I have not been pursuing."

'If I order in, will you eat please? If you keep avoiding food and losing weight, there won't be much of you for me to see."

"I'll do it for you." She found it hard to believe that this man with so much compassion and kindness could be the man that the gossip at Mercy Seat portrayed him to be. She liked everything about Jehu, right down to the way he ate his salad, and not mixing his foods on his plate. He didn't gobble his food or make those awful smacking sounds, like Candace. She hoped that whatever she didn't know about him was also good. But she had to know the truth.

Is he really on the down low or is it just a rumor. Oh God, don't let it be true.

CHAPTER TWENTY-EIGHT

The feeling of butterflies fluttering crowded her stomach. This was Jessica's first day back at Mercy Seat and she wasn't sure she wanted to be there. The stares of the congregation were not unusual, but she wondered if there was some gossip about her and King.

Reverend Anderson's sermon was just what she needed. He always had a word of encouragement; inspiring her to continue her plight to find out who Jesus really is. As she was leaving the church, she was close enough to Reverend Ben to hear his conversation with a young lady leaving out.

"Hello, I'm Reverend Ben, Assistant Pastor. Thank you for joining us today," he said, reaching out to shake her hand.

"I'm Melanie Brown. I'm pleased to meet you."

"I hope you will visit us again soon," he said, holding her right hand and placing his left hand on top.

Jessica could see that familiar flirtatious look in Reverend Ben's eyes. The line of people exiting the church was getting longer and it was noticeable that he was taking longer with his greeting to her.

"I look forward to you joining us next week," he said releasing her hand and turning his attention to the couple behind her.

As much as Jessica wanted to avoid him, there was no way she could get out of the line without everyone seeing her. Before she could find an escape route, she was eye to eye with him.

"Sister Jessica, it's so good to see you."

"And you as well," Jessica replied, quickly shaking his hand and moving forward.

The anger grew inside her as she walked toward her car thinking of how his actions had caused the loss of her friendship with Candace. She turned her attention to the fast steps of high heel shoes quickly approaching her from behind.

"Jessica, Jessica, wait up. I need to talk to you," Candace said, taking short breaths. She caught up with Jessica and they walked side by side.

"I know I'm the last person you want to talk to Jessica, but I want to apologize and ask your forgiveness."

Jessica continued walking. She wasn't sure she was ready to forgive Candace. The replay of all the days Candace ignored her and embarrassed her kept flashing through her mind.

"Jessica, I was wrong. I let my desperation blind me to the truth. You were right. No man is worth losing our friendship over." Candace picked up her pace until she was able to come face to face with Jessica.

"Please forgive me. I miss you."

Jessica saw the face of the young girl she had known since they were teenagers. This was the look she remembered when they vowed to be best friends forever. Forgiveness was one of the things that she remembered from Reverend Anderson's teachings. She recalled him saying that if you want God to forgive you, you need to forgive others. With all the things she needed forgiveness for, now would be a good time to start a forgiveness account with God. She burst into laughter, threw her arms around Candace and gave her a big hug.

"Alright Holy Mama, I'll forgive you, but on one condition."

"And what's that?" Candace said, wiping the tears from her eyes.

"You have to take me out for fried chicken."

"You want to go to Mandy's, the best fried chicken place in town?" Candace smiled and Jessica saw the friend that she always remembered.

"Absolutely, I wouldn't settle for anything less," Jessica said giving Candace another hug.

There was no need to look at the menu. Jessica knew exactly what she wanted. "I'll have fried chicken with dressing, greens, candied sweets, and mac and cheese. Oh, and peach cobbler with ice cream for dessert," Jessica told the waitress.

"This is for your friend, right? So what's your order?" the waitress said, looking at Jessica.

"No, that's for me," Jessica smiled.

"So what are you having?" the waitress said to Candace.

"Ditto," Candace replied.

"Are you two playing games with me today? Because if you are, I'm much too busy for your jokes."

"Oh no, Hattie, we would never do that to you. Jessica and I are celebrating."

"I have this great appetite because I haven't eaten in a few days," Jessica laughed.

"So would you like a pitcher of iced tea instead of a glass?" Hattie said, looking at one, then the other.

"Yes and plenty of lemons also, Jessica said." They both laughed as Hattie walked away waving both hands in the air. They stared at each other for a few minutes. The pain of a broken relationship was something they never wanted to experience again.

"I saw Reverend Ben in action today Jessica," Candace said, breaking the silence.

"Yes, and I was close enough to hear him in action. I wanted to tell the whole church about how he hides behind that robe pretending to be fishing for souls when he's actually just throwing out the bait to see who will bite."

"I can't believe I got fooled like that and played right into his hands. I feel so stupid."

"It's okay Candace. Some of the best of us get fooled. It's difficult to see things as they are when you are standing in the middle of the situation. Sometimes you have to step back and get a better view of things."

"You mean like King Jordan?" She looked toward the entrance. King was making his grand entrance as he always did, greeting everyone. When he approached Jessica and Candace, he paused long enough to say hello and moved on to be seated.

"What is it with you two? He's usually all smiles and roaming eyes when he's in your presence Jessica."

"Let's just say I met the real King Jordan."

"You mean the one that reels you in with the pretense of helping you grow in Christ, gets your trust, and then attacks you like a sly pit bull before you're aware of what's happening?"

"Candace, you mean you really did have a fling with King? Why didn't you tell me?"

"Jessica I tried to warn you, but you wouldn't listen. I was too ashamed to tell you the truth. I just prayed that you would wise up to him. I'm so sorry Jessica. You have every right to be upset with me. It looks like I'll spend the rest of the day asking you to forgive me."

"Is there something else that you need to tell me while you're on a roll?"

"Well–uh, yes. Jehu and I had a few dates."

Jessica picked up her purse and stood up to leave. She asked the question and she got an answer that she didn't want to hear.

"But I swear Jessica, he was a perfect gentleman." She grabbed Jessica by the hand. "I thought he was on the down low and just using me as a cover. He kept trying to tell me what the word of God says about sex outside of marriage and I just didn't want to hear it."

"You mean you really don't know if he's sincere about living according to God's word or if he is really gay? Jessica was still standing, not sure if she wanted to stick around to hear more of Candace's explanation.

"No, I really don't and if you really care about him, I suggest you find out. Don't make the mistake of listening to me and others who are ashamed to say that they went out with the fine brother and didn't get any sex. Keep in mind that the gossip club is only passing along what they have heard."

Jessica sat down slowly looking at Candace and shaking her head. She didn't know if she should be angry or glad she now knew the truth. "I'll give it some thought." A smile came over her face. "He is a nice fine brother, saved and smells good. I'm not sure any of these men are worth the salt that goes in their bread." Candace joined in with Jessica on the last part of her comment as if she anticipated what she was about to say.

"My mama used that phrase all the time," Candace recalled, raising her voice.

"I thought my grandmother coined that phrase," Jessica said, "but I guess not. I suppose it's been passed down through the generations." They both laughed heartily and for a moment it was just like old times.

"So this is what it feels like when you forgive. You feel free, like you've released a heavy load of something. Don't you agree Candace?"

"Um hu," Candace remarked chewing.

"Candace, what are you eating? You must have a hole in your stomach. I bet you had breakfast and—"

"Okay ladies, here's your feast," Hattie said, pushing the cart closer to the table. "For the lady who never orders fried chicken, here you go. And for the lady who always orders fried chicken, bon appetite, or something like that." Candace and Jessica laughed and Hattie joined in.

"I declare you ladies are on a silly ride today and trying to take me with you. Can I get you anything else?"

"Not at the moment," Jessica answered.

"Alright, I'll check on you later."

Candace dug into her food as if she was at the table alone and all you could hear was the sound of her chewing. Jessica was happy that reconciliation was on the table for them. She loved Candace like a sister and truly wanted to stay friends forever, but she couldn't help but wonder if Candace had more little secrets she was hiding.

CHAPTER TWENTY-NINE

Jessica hesitated at the front door of the church while she pondered whether she was making a mistake by meeting with Millie. After the way she embarrassed her in front of the entire Sunday school class and from the conversation she overheard in the ladies room, she was convinced that Millie was not trying to help her. She entered the church and walked down the long hall and opened the door to the training classroom. Millie stood up from the desk to greet her.

"Thank you for coming Jessica. Please be seated. I'll get right to the point. I haven't been very supportive of you or sensitive to the things that you have been facing here at Mercy Seat. I feel bad about the role I have played in some of the situations you have endured here. I know this will be difficult for you to believe, but I understand what you have been going through because I once encountered the same type of rejection and temptation that I know you have been experiencing. One day I was driving by the church and read the sign out front. I didn't even notice the Seat part of the sign at first; it was almost like it was invisible. I only saw the word Mercy. I didn't even know what mercy meant, but it sounded like something I needed. Then I read the marquee that said *God wants to heal all of your hurts*. I knew without a doubt that I needed healing. When I came to Mercy Seat I was messed up, abused and misused. I sat in the back of the church listening and watching. No one had ever done anything to cause me to trust them; therefore, I was skeptical of everyone. I had been through so much in my lifetime that what I encountered here at Mercy Seat was not a big deal for me. I didn't know how to deal with the challenges, so I just ignored them. Once I married Daniel, people started to treat me better. I began to read and study the word of God and it changed me. I was able to minister to others and help them understand the word of God. I was doing fine until Daniel's accident and the anger and bitterness that I hadn't dealt with resurfaced. Jessica I saw myself in you and I hated what I saw. I wanted to help you, but I had too much anger and bitterness in me. God showed me that until I dealt with my own issues, I couldn't help others. My husband was really instrumental in helping me to see the real me, and through prayer God has delivered me from the anger and bitterness that was keeping me from being the vessel that God has called me to be. Will you forgive me Jessica and will you allow me to help you?"

Millie was doing something that she had never done before in her life; asking for forgiveness and admitting she was wrong. As she spoke, she could feel something changing inside her. She wasn't quite sure what was happening, but she knew the Spirit of the Lord was working in her. It was the fear of what people would think of her, especially Daniel, that had hindered her from confessing before now. She wasn't sure why she chose Jessica to confess to, but she knew that revealing the secrets that had kept her bound all these years would help to set her free.

Jessica was astonished by Millie's confession. Millie and others at Mercy Seat had purposely made her life a living hell and she was still very angry. Millie waited patiently for her to respond. Jessica leaned back in her chair and looked away from Millie as she searched her mind for something to say.

This is another difficult decision God. I need you. Please tell me what to do.

"Millie", she said after a few moments of silence. "I don't know what to say. This forgiveness thing is so new to me. It's so hard for me to say yes. I know God wants me to forgive, but I believe he also wants me to be sincere about it. Right now Millie, I'm not feeling very sincere."

"I understand Jessica. Nobody knows better than me how difficult it is to forgive. One of my biggest struggles was to forgive myself. I have been held captive by my own fears and unforgiveness. I'm sharing this with you because I want you to be made whole too. I believe my testimony can help you to overcome your issues. I pray that God will help you to forgive me." She paused then continued. "I have another reason for wanting to meet with you. I want to give you another opportunity to teach the class again. Can you be ready by next week?"

"I'm not sure I'm worthy to teach God's word."

"But are you willing? You've been studying and preparing, so now are you willing to do what God has called you to do? Just say yes to the Lord

Jessica," Millie urged, reaching out for Jessica's hand. Jessica could hear Reverend Anderson's teaching on forgiveness as clear as if he was right in the room. *"If you want God to forgive you for your sins, then you must forgive others. It's not always easy, but it's possible and rewarding. You'll be able to move forward in peace to do the things that God has called you to do for his Kingdom."*

Millie was displaying compassion that Jessica would never have believed she was capable of if she hadn't been experiencing it first-hand. She thought her reservoir of tears had dried up, but obviously the reserve had kicked in. This was definitely a Kodak moment, Jessica and Millie embracing and releasing their pinned up emotions.

CHAPTER THIRTY

Jessica prayed that today would not be a repeat of her first attempt to teach the Sunday school class. To be humiliated again would be devastating. She really wanted to believe that Millie was sincere in her apology, but her previous actions still left some doubt in Jessica's mind. She took another look at herself in the mirror. All eyes would be on her today for more than one reason. She wanted to make sure that her dress would not be a negative topic of conversation.

"You're looking good girl. I think even God approves," she said, taking a last glance in the mirror before heading out the door.

She arrived early to get set up and pull her nerves together. Millie was already there waiting for her, suggesting they have prayer. Jessica couldn't believe that things were off to such a good start.

"Good morning Jessica," Naomi said, "It's good to see you. Are you finally teaching today?"

"Yes I am," Jessica responded.

"That's wonderful," Naomi said. Anita nodded her head in agreement. They both rolled their eyes in the direction of Millie and sat down as if they were preparing to give Jessica their undivided attention. They usually chewed gum and whispered throughout the class. There was no reason to believe that today would be different.

"Good morning class," Jessica spoke out. Everyone echoed a good morning back to her.

"Last week we were in the book of Genesis. We talked about how Joseph's brothers sold him into slavery because they were jealous of him. Today we're going to discuss how he dealt with his unjust incarceration. We'll discuss the things Joseph endured as God prepared him for his true purpose for the kingdom and what we can learn from his life."

Jessica knew God was with her when she began to feel confident in what she was saying. She glanced back at Millie who surprisingly gave her a nod of approval. Jehu sat with a smile on his face reassuring her that she was on the right track. He kept his word and came to support her.

"In the book of Genesis, chapter 39," Jessica continued, "Joseph was brought to the house of Potiphar, an officer of Pharaoh, and was made overseer of his house. Potiphar's wife began to make advances toward Joseph and plotted to lure him into her chambers. Does that sound familiar to any of you sisters?"

"Absolutely," Naomi and Anita agreed as a few others joined in with them.

"But Joseph resisted her and one day as he was running away from her, she grabbed his coat and used it as evidence to support her lies that he attacked her. Joseph was thrown into jail for something that he didn't do. How do you think Joseph felt knowing that he was innocent and even though God was with him, it didn't keep him from being locked up?

"I think Joseph had a lot of faith that God would help him through this," brother Amos slowly spoke out.

"I would probably be upset with God," Clara said, standing up with a frown on her face. "If

God loved Joseph so much, why did he allow all those bad things to happen to him? I don't know if I will ever understand why God allows bad things to happen to us. I think……"

"Well Clara," Anita cut in, "If you make it to heaven, you can ask God." She and Naomi snickered.

"Thank you all for your comments," Jessica said, attempting to get back on focus. What do you think it's like to be incarcerated and know that you're innocent, but can't prove it? Can you imagine being locked up for something you didn't do without any witnesses on your side? How would you feel about that injustice and—"

Melvin, who never spoke a word in class, but would make a grunting sound if he disagreed with something or a high pitched moan if he agreed, stood up and began to speak before Jessica finished.

"I think I would begin to lose faith in God if I couldn't see his purpose in my being locked up. I would feel abandoned." He quickly sat down.

"But Brother Melvin," said Mother Eleanor. "We don't always know what God's purpose is for allowing things to happen to us, but we must believe that his word is true. His word says that he will never leave us or forsake us. It has to be hard to believe that you have not been forsaken if you are locked up for something you didn't do, but Jesus suffered and died on the cross for you and me and he was guilty of nothing. The result is that we have access to heaven. You must have faith in God."

Brother Melvin grunted and folded his arms. Jessica could see Millie squirming in her seat as the discussion continued. Millie raised her hand to be recognized to speak. Jessica feared that her teaching was about to become another embarrassing moment. Millie walked to the front of the class and began to speak.

"Being incarcerated and knowing you are innocent is very difficult. Incarceration is not limited to just being in jail; you can be locked up in life's situations that keep you bound. I was locked up in an abusive lifestyle through no fault of my own. As a young child I was mentally and sexually abused; and the abuse continued through my adulthood with different people," Millie said. "One day I just couldn't take it anymore and in the midst of getting my head banged against a wall, I stabbed my husband to death. When I finally got the nerve to fight back, I landed in jail. Now that is injustice." Tears filled her eyes and slowly rolled down her face. No one at Mercy Seat had ever seen the sensitive side of Millie, other than Jessica. She composed herself and looked around the class and then looked upward as if to make sure God was with her before she continued.

"It has taken me over twenty years to admit this to anyone. Until I came to Mercy Seat, incarceration was a way of life for me."

Although she had never been to jail, Jessica could empathize with Millie. She had been locked in a self-destructive routine of meeting the same type of men with different names, but all with the same agenda for her life. It was always a road that left her feeling empty, unloved and alone. Coming to Mercy Seat just added to her resume of failures and pain, but somehow she felt this was the place where she could change her life and get free.

The silence in the car on the way home from church was like a loud gong repeatedly sounding in Millie's ears. She couldn't read Daniel's mind, but she could feel his anger. He always cleared his throat before he spoke when he was angry, but today he continuously cleared his throat and remained silent. Millie had never experienced Daniel's silence. It had always been her that shut him out, but now that the table was turned, she was probably feeling the pain and neglect that she had inflicted on him all these years. The truth was out and she had to tell him the whole story, when he was ready to listen. How would she tell him? Where would she start?

Oh God, only you can get me through this mess. I'm calling on you. You said you would answer if I call. Can you answer right now Lord?

As she pulled into the drive way, she glanced over at Daniel and saw something that cut to the core of her heart. She had never seen him cry.

CHAPTER THIRTY-ONE

The melodious sounds of the church choir filled the church. Everyone turned when Millie and Daniel entered the sanctuary. Daniel wheeled himself to the front of the church with the other deacons. Millie took her usual seat and ignored the stares from the congregation. This was just another hurdle that she had to conquer. Although she tried, Daniel was still in a silent mode, speaking only when necessary.

The church clerk walked to the podium to make the announcements. "We have a very special announcement today. Would Reverend Benjamin Rogers and Sarita Noble please stand?"

Reverend Ben gestured for the clerk to hand him the microphone.

"I'm excited," Reverend Ben said with a big grin. "Sarita Noble has accepted my proposal of marriage. Would my beautiful wife to be please stand?

Show then your ring honey. Sarita stood and held up her finger to show off her one carat engagement ring.

"We would like to invite the congregation to our wedding. We haven't agreed on a date yet, but it will be soon and held here at Mercy Seat."

You could hear whispers and comments throughout the church as most of the congregation applauded.

"My congratulations to Reverend Ben and Sarita," Reverend Anderson said, initiating another applause from the congregation. "I'd like to see more weddings here at Mercy Seat, especially from those of you who have been in long term relationships. Remember brothers, when you find a wife, you find a good thing. Amen?" A few brothers responded.

"There is more good news. The testimony of one of our long standing members has begun an outpouring of phone calls to my office in the past week. The word of God in the book of Revelation 12:11 says, 'And they overcame him by the blood of the Lamb, and by the word of their testimony'......

Sister Millie McKay has put aside her pride and revealed a very personal aspect of her life. Now she can begin to experience complete freedom and receive all of the blessings that God has for her. Because many of you that phoned to say that Sister Millie's testimony inspired you to want to overcome your own issues, I have decided to start a new class called The Joseph Group. I'm going to ask Sister Millie to be in charge of getting that class started. I expect all of you that called to be among the first to sign up for this class. I'm sure there are many more who didn't call that need to sign up as well. It is so important that we don't allow the enemy to keep a foothold on our lives so that we may grow in the word of God to become all that he wants us to be. Amen?" "Amen," the congregation responded.

"Choir, give us one of those inspiring songs."

While the choir sang, Reverend Anderson scanned his congregation. He tried to imagine how many of his members lives were on hold because they were carrying unresolved issues that required God's intervention. Men and women who, day after day, have pushed years of pain further back in their memory as they tried to forget them, not realizing that it only hardened their hearts and delayed their blessings.

CHAPTER THIRTY-TWO

Millie wasn't sure how much more she could take of Daniel's silence. It was worse than all the hurt he had caused her in the past. An occasional yes or thank you was the extent of their conversation. She had been praying for a breakthrough and hoped that Reverend Anderson's announcement to the church and the support shown from some of the members would move him to communicate with her. They were in the middle of dinner, when her prayer was answered.

"Millie", Daniel said. "I know my silence has been challenging for you, but it has not been easy for me either."

Millie laid her fork aside and leaned back in her chair to listen to Daniel.

"I realize it has been difficult for you to care for me and not have the companionship that you deserve in a marriage," he continued. In light of your recent testimony, I feel you should not have to suffer through this marriage any longer. I'm offering you your freedom so that you can live the kind of life that you deserve."

"Daniel," Millie tried to interrupt.

"No Millie, let me finish. You sacrificed much to take care of me. I'll do right by you in the divorce settlement. I'm willing to set up a bank account for you so that you will be able to take care of yourself until you find work and still have a savings. I can hire a live in care giver. The divorce will be quick because we will both agree. We can talk about other things that you want included in the settlement. I love you Millie, that's why I want the best for you. You still have a lot of good years left. Go live them and let God bring someone into your life that can make you happy."

Millie sat speechless looking at Daniel. Although he had caused her much grief, he had brought much joy in her life in the early years of their relationship. She never dreamed that she would attract such a good looking man with substance. He had a reputation as a Casanova, but she fell in love with him and he chose her over all the others. Her past life before meeting Daniel had been sheltered. He taught her how to survive in the church and in the community. He convinced her to go back to school and get her GED. Her level of self-esteem took a positive turn and she began to believe that she could do some good things with her life. This would not be a good time for her to abandon him when he really needed her? Millie pushed her chair away from the table and walked over to Daniel and knelt beside him.

"Daniel I really haven't been very kind to you since your accident. I was hurt and even embarrassed because the entire church knew the circumstances surrounding the accident; but we've had some good years together and you have been good to me. Will you forgive me Daniel?" Millie said, laying her head on Daniel's lap.

"I forgave you long ago Millie," Daniel responded, stroking Millie's hair. "I love you enough to let you go. You will never have the kind of intimacy that you want with me. Can't you understand that?"

"No Daniel, I won't leave you. We can get through this. I will work harder at being a better wife and we'll start doing some enjoyable things together like we used to do. Intimacy is about more than just sex. I love you and leaving you is not going to change that. Remember, one of the doctors told you that it is a possibility that your paralysis could be reversed, but in my state of anger, I have constantly told you that it would never happen. I was so wrong to put that doubt in your spirit. I kept my past life a secret from you all these years and it was not my intention to tell the world before I told you. To be honest, it was not something that I ever intended to share with anyone. Will you allow me to tell you the whole truth Daniel? I don't want any more secrets between us. Let's agree in the word for your healing and our marriage. Let's try Daniel. Let's at least try," Millie cried.

Daniel knew Millie was right. It was her constantly reminding him that he was less than a man and telling him that God was punishing him for his infidelity that made him start doubting God for his healing. God was not going to heal him as long as he didn't believe that he would. He reached over and put his hand on Millie's chin, raised her head and looked into her eyes.

"Millie, I love you too and I don't want to lose you. But I don't want you to continue to be unhappy."

"How about if we get some counseling from Reverend Anderson, and talk to the doctors and physical therapists again," Millie said. "If we don't try, we will never know what God will do."

"Are you sure you want to do this Millie?"

"Yes, Daniel, I'm sure."

"If you're willing then so am I. As long as there is life, there is hope. We'll trust God and pray for a miracle."

"Yes Daniel, that is exactly what we will do," she said as they embraced.

CHAPTER THIRTY-THREE

"You wouldn't have to ring my bell and wait to get in. I would just give you your own key."

Jehu turned to the pretty smiling face of the lady that he had encountered on the night he was pleading for Jessica to let him in.

"Remember me? If things don't work out, I'm Betty in apartment 605, code 201," she said dangling her keys in the air as she entered the door. Jehu smiled at her the way he knew would capture a woman's attention. That's the smile that often got him into trouble. He knew it was working when she stopped and turned around without speaking and waited for him to respond.

The door opened behind him.

"Jehu, I'm so sorry. I got stuck in traffic and I didn't expect you to be early," Jessica said. I tried calling, but it kept going to voicemail."

"It's okay, I've only been here a few minutes," he said, giving her a kiss on the cheek. He glanced over his shoulder to see the elevator door closing.

He had given a lot of thought to what he wanted to say to Jessica, but now that he was with her, he no longer felt that brave impulse to be honest with her. Decisions usually came easy for him and whenever they didn't turn out to be the best decisions, he was always willing to deal with the consequences of his actions. He was attracted to Jessica the very first time he saw her and he felt bad that his silence had added to her roller coaster ride at Mercy Seat. He was sure that she had been plagued with the church gossip about him and the rumors became even more believable each time he turned down her advances. He knew that other men in the church were throwing their hooks out for Jessica, especially King Jordan. He wanted to ask her why they seemed to be avoiding each other recently, but since King was turning his attention to the new girl in the choir, maybe he was no longer a threat to their relationship.

Once they were in her apartment, Jessica quickly refreshed herself, combed her hair and changed into a pair of jeans and tee shirt. She wasn't sure why Jehu wanted an audience with her, but she was glad he came. He was sitting on the sofa sipping a glass of ginger ale when she entered the room.

"I hope you don't mind, I made one for you also."

"I'm glad that you feel comfortable enough to do that. Sorry for leaving you so long, but I wanted to get into something comfortable."

"I understand," he said handing her a glass of ginger ale. He knew that telling Jessica the truth could mean losing her for good; however, not telling her the truth could bring the same result. He loved Jessica and it was probably time to break the silence and be upfront with her. He moved closer to her and sat his glass on the table in front of them.

"I love you Jessica. Do you love me? He knew the answer could possibly be no and he could be hurt again.

Jessica looked at him in surprise. She paused before answering him. She had learned never to say yes unless you know it's to your benefit. "I've been very upfront about my feelings for you Jehu. Do you doubt that?"

"I need to know if you love me Jessica," he said, pressing her for an answer.

What if I tell him I love him, she thought, *and he tells me that he's been on the down low, but he believes God will deliver him? I'm not waiting for him to be delivered. Furthermore, I'm not sure I want to be with a man who would admit that he desires other men.*

"I don't know if you have been honest with me Jehu. The rumors at Mercy Seat are so wide spread until I don't know what to believe. Now is the time for you to make a believer out of me."

He looked into her eyes. "Jessica, I have always had women chasing after me and in the past I took advantage of many of them. I hurt a great number of people along the way, but since I gave my life to Jesus, that part of my life is over. About four years ago, I met someone that I wanted to have a serious relationship with and she hurt me. The word of God was the only comfort I could find and it showed me that I needed to change my lifestyle and be obedient to God. I made some mistakes on this journey for the Lord, but I refuse to quit. Whenever I do something contrary to God's word, I feel convicted and that is very painful. I've learned to ask God for forgiveness and believe that he does.

I dated a few women at Mercy Seat and they all expected me to go to bed with them. When I didn't, they assumed the worst. This is how the rumor started that I'm either gay or on the down low. I have been abstaining from sex and praying God will send someone into my life that will agree to walk in obedience with me; allow me to court her and build a relationship that would lead to marriage. I would like that person to be you." He waited for her to respond.

Jessica's tongue felt as if it was stuck to the roof of her mouth. Her heart leaped for joy. This is just what she had prayed for many years, someone to court her and be honest with her, but she had no idea that not having sex would be a part of this dream.

Jehu's heart pounded fast. He silently prayed that telling Jessica the truth had not been a mistake. He had just told her the secret that no one but his mother and God knew. The journey of abstinence had been tough and one that he couldn't walk without lots of prayer and fasting. He kept a small spiritual devotional in his brief case, glove compartment and at the office. He never wanted to be without the word to remind him when temptation came knocking. He had begun to understand what Paul meant in the book of Romans by being transformed by the renewing of your mind. He had to limit the time he spent with old friends and even sever some friendship. He used to be the life of the party, but now he spent most of his time with the Singles Ministry, and reading and studying the Bible.

"Jehu," Jessica said, snapping him out of his thoughts. "I'm not sure I can abstain from sex for long periods of time. I'm not strong enough to do that."

"I'll help you. We can study the word, fast and pray together. We can be accountable to each other, being careful not to do things that we know can be tempting. There is a certain joy that comes with being obedient to God. You're not convinced that God answers prayers, but I know that he does. Will you at least try?"

Jessica believed he was sincere. She loved him and really wanted to have an intimate relationship with him. "I'd love to have a relationship with you, but how long is this courtship supposed to last; and then what?"

"God has helped me to abstain for almost two years. I'm certainly hoping that I won't have to go another two. I believe that through prayer and trusting God, He will give us the direction we need and help us determine the right time to marry."

Jessica let out a long heavy sigh. "I need some time to think about this Jehu. Okay?"

"Sure, I understand, but I hope you won't take too long. Please pray about it."

"I will, because I need to know for myself that God answers prayer. This will be a good opportunity for me to find out."

CHAPTER THIRTY-FOUR

It was a perfect day for a June wedding; warm, clear blue skies, a mild breeze and no humidity. The people were gathering in the church for Candace's wedding and Jessica was happy for her as the wedding party was slowly coming in. She wanted to make sure Candace was ready for the photographer to take pictures, but when she opened the door, Candace was sitting there staring at herself in the mirror.

"Candace, why aren't you dressed? The photographer is here and soon your husband to be will be standing at the altar and you are not ready." Jessica stopped abruptly when she noticed the sad look on Candace face.

"Candace, what's wrong?"

"I'm not sure I can do this Jessica. I feel like I'm stuck to this stool. My heart feels like it's going to run away and leave me," Candace said slowly.

"Why, ah—why don't I tell the photographer that you're having wardrobe challenges and you need a few extra minutes? Ok Candace?"

"Yea, yea, okay," Candace said reluctantly.

Jessica returned to Candace and sat beside her. "Now tell me Holy Mama, what's really bothering you?"

"I'm not sure I'm ready to wake up to Albert every morning. I'm so accustomed to doing my own thing whenever I want to and now I have to change. Now is the time to back out. Once I say I do, it will be final. Right Jessica?"

"That's right Candace. It will be final. But don't you love Albert?"

"Yes, of course I do," Candace said without hesitation.

"That's good," Jessica continued. "Do you love him enough to want to have him in your life until death comes between you?"

"Jessica that sounds so cold and final. I'm accustomed to having him come and go at my will and if we marry, he will always be there. I'm afraid I won't make a good wife." Tears filled her eyes.

"But Candace, you were out of God's will when you were having it your way. Isn't that what Reverend Anderson is always teaching us, to stay in the will of God? Candace, don't cry. You'll ruin your make up and your dress. You've had your counseling with Reverend Anderson and that went well. Right?"

"Yes," she sniffled.

"Is there something that you didn't discuss that needed to be discussed?"

"Yes, my fears," Candace mumbled.

"Candace, do you want to spend more years looking for Mr. Right when he's waiting for you right now? Do you want more days of feeling sorry for yourself, disappointments, or to be hanging out with me on those special days that you could be with your husband? Do you want to grow old by yourself?"

"No, I don't want to grow old alone Jessica. Will you help me finish getting ready to meet my husband?"

Candace prepared to take pictures and then join her uncle for the walk down the aisle. Jessica hoped that she had said the right things. She knew what fear was like, although she'd never felt what Candace was experiencing.

Jessica prayed believing that God would hear her for Candace's sake.

Oh God, Jessica silently prayed. *Help my sister Candace. Step in between her and the enemy. Help her to do the right thing today.*

"Candace, your uncle Fred is waiting to escort you down the aisle to take your vows. Come on, you can do this. I'll be down front praying for you."

"You praying? That's worth walking down the aisle for," Candace said laughing.

The wedding party stood waiting for the ceremony to begin. The groomsmen wore big bold striped ties and the bridesmaids wore pastel colored dresses that matched the stripes in their bow ties.

Albert stood beside his best man in his black tuxedo and a bow tie with the same striped pattern as his groomsmen. You could see his right foot tapping up and down. Jessica laughed inside remembering Candace's comment that she hoped she didn't have any boys because Albert would want colored pampers and matching outfits. One colorfully dressed man in her life was enough.

The ceremony began and the bridal party started down the aisle. Then it was Jessica's turn as the maid of honor. The diamond earrings that Keith had given her looked perfect with her cream colored, sleeveless, straight fitted dress with a V-neck cut in the back. Her shoes were light gold beaded three inch heels. She wondered how she would feel when her turn came to take that walk down the aisle as a bride.

Candace was a beautiful bride. She wore a white mermaid dress with drop shoulders that accented her perfect petite body. Her veil was trimmed in miniature pearls and her ears were adorned with tear-dropped pearl earrings. The sexy three inch, pearl beaded strappy sandals exposed her French manicured toes. She held a bouquet of yellow calla lilies. Albert had a smile on his face that seemed to be painted on, but everyone knew that it was genuine. Candace still couldn't believe that she had made it down the aisle and was standing beside Albert. The itching in her feet to make a run for it finally stopped when she saw the smile on Albert's face and the love in his eyes for her that she knew was real. When she heard Reverend Anderson say, "By the power invested in me by the state of Illinois, I now pronounce you man and wife. Albert, you may salute your bride," she knew this was final and she was no longer free and single. She gave Jessica a quick wink as Albert followed Reverend Anderson's directions.

"I now present to you for the first time Mr. and Mrs. Albert Connors."

Seeing Candace get married was encouraging to Jessica. Jehu joined her in the reception line. He gently squeezed her hand and smiled, as if to say you're next. It was dance time and he picked a slow dance. It gave Jessica a chance to get close to him and smell that familiar fragrance she loved so much.

Lord you have got to be kidding me. Getting this close to this fine man and just smelling him is all I get unless I marry him? If you're not with me on this one, I'm in big trouble.

"Mr. and Mrs. Albert Connors sounds good, doesn't it Jessica?"

"Yes it does; almost as good as Mr. and Mrs. Jehu Edwards." He stopped in the middle of the dance.

"Does that mean that you have made a decision about us and we can look forward to planning our own wedding in the near future?"

She looked at Jehu and hesitated before answering him. She knew that she loved him and he had all of the qualities that she wanted in a man. He certainly was more than she had ever hoped for considering the men that flowed through her life before him. He had also convinced her that God does answer prayers.

"Yes Mr. Smelling Good, that's exactly what it means. But I expect those plans to be real soon."

He kissed her as if she had just said I do.

"It will be Jessica. I promise, it will be.

Oh God, I hope you're on duty today!

Dear Readers:

Thank you for reading Subtle Deceit. I hope you enjoyed it. Let me know if you are interested in a sequel. Would you like to know?

1. Did Jessica make another bad choice with Jehu?
2. Can Jehu really help Jessica get over Keith or is there still a crack in the door?
3. Will Keith continue to pursue Jessica?
4. Is Jehu really on the down low?
5. Will Jehu and Jessica get married?
6. Are there more secrets Candace is keeping from Jessica?
7. Will Candace make a good wife or will her quest for the ideal guy hinder her relationship with Albert?
8. Will King find a good mate or will he remain true to his reputation as a womanizer?
9. Will Millie stay committed to Daniel or will she meet someone that causes her to have a change of heart?
10. Will Jessica make a real commitment to her relationship with Jesus Christ?

Please contact me on Alma Davey FACE BOOK. I look forward to your comments.